Battling Monsters and Other F'd Up Dates

THE GRIMM BROTHERHOOD
BOOK THREE

KEL CARPENTER

WITH
MEG ANNE

 Created with Vellum

For Karma, the fiercest protector, most loyal friend, and purest soul I've ever known. The world lost some of its magic the day you said goodbye.

I'm Death, and I make sure that everyone is equal.

— THE BROTHERS GRIMM

Hunted

WHAT THE ACTUAL FUCK?

My heart beat in erratic rhythms as my doppelgänger lifted her Ray-Bans and my own gray eyes stared back.

I wish I had something clever to say. I'd like to think that I could handle this craziness with the same laissez-faire attitude I approached life with.

But let's be real. This is me we're talking about.

Hammer meet nail.

"Who the fuck are you?" I demanded, crossing my arms over my chest.

"My name is Thana," she said, striding forward with a sleek gait. "Daughter of Death."

It was eerie to see my own body move with the litheness of a predator. My eyebrows drew together as my thoughts started whirring.

There was a moment there where I heard her words, but they didn't really compute with my short-circuiting brain. I was either in shock or having a seizure.

Judging by the continued stream of consciousness,

shock was winning. Though I wasn't willing to rule anything out just yet.

"But *I'm* the Daughter of Death—" I started. For some reason, it was the 'Daughter of Death' comment that snagged my attention the most. While I didn't even know what it meant to be one, I was already territorial of my title.

I mean, I did just save, like, *all* the reapers from death.

Being a supe freak was now my schtick.

I didn't know who this gray-haired broad was, but until I did, I was going to pull one from Esme's book. Stick to my guns. Or in this case, my foul mouth and charming personality.

"And my sister," she said, finishing my sentence, though not the way I would have expected. "*My* twin." Her gaze drifted over my shoulder to where Shepard's ghost was hovering. She gave him a pointed look before looking to me once more.

"I don't understand," I said slowly. "I don't have a sister."

Even if I did have a doppelgänger. Weird. Next level kind of weird.

Like some *Twilight Zone* shit.

"You did," she said, but it came out closer to a purr. She leaned forward and lifted one of my pale pink locks, twirling it in her finger. "Before you were reborn."

Up to that point, time was moving slower for me. My thoughts were tripping over one another, trying to come up with who the fuck this girl was. I mean, she looked like me, she dressed like me, if it weren't for her corporeal form—I might have thought I was hallucinating. Maybe *I* accidentally split a piece of my soul—just like James.

But here she was, a second version of myself standing in the flesh.

The idea of having another twin seemed crazy . . . until you remembered the little tiny fact that apparently I reincarnated.

Was it possible that a past version of me, wasn't just me?

I looked at Shep. "You're seeing this too, right?"

Some of the seriousness drained from my brother's face as he gave me an annoyed twist of his lips, followed by a very dramatic sigh. "Yes, Salem, I see her too."

"Just checking," I muttered.

Sheesh. You'd think for being dead, he'd be less irritable since I was going to bring him back. Fucker.

Least I wasn't hallucinating. That much was clear.

"I can assure you, I'm quite real, Salem. I know this is probably a shock to you, and you've always been a bit unpredictable when given surprises, but there's no other way to really say this." She took a deep breath, and all I could think about was the fact that this was not how I planned to spend my morning. I was starting to wish I'd never left the pool house, which was crazy, because you'd think that I would want to know if I had a twin running around, right? Well. That was probably the shock. Hostess cupcakes were really good at getting someone over shock, though. "You and I were the original Daughters of Death in this realm," Thana announced, putting an end to my meandering. Her next words were an icy bucket of water over my head. "*We* created the reapers. *We* maintained the order in the supernatural world. You and I."

I opened and closed my mouth, eventually settling on the most important and obvious questions.

"What happened, then?" I asked. "Why was I killed? *How* was I killed?"

"A monster." Her eyes flashed with cold fury. I felt the chill from it deep inside.

"A monster?" I repeated, not letting my unease show. I used my dubious tone of voice and narrowed my eyes.

"From the realm of death," she said. "It's been hunting us. After your first death, we were separated, and it took many years to find you. By then it was too late. You died again. This happened several times along the way. But I've found you now . . ." Her words trailed off as she released the lock of hair and cupped my cheek. "We'll be together again. I've grown over the centuries. My power has grown. I can keep you safe where others cannot." Her skin was cool to the touch. Her expression genuine. Sincere.

"How did you find me?"

"Death," she said simply. "I felt your presence enter the spirit realm. There's only one person who is my equal in everything. I knew it was you."

Well, that seemed to make sense. As much as any of this did.

It was a lot to take in, though. Something niggled in the back of my brain. Like she wasn't telling me the complete truth.

"You've been in town for a little while now," I said, shaking off her hand. She had no outward reaction. No surprise. No hurt at my movement. Nothing.

The inhumanness of her reactions, the way she oscillated from sincere to cold so rapidly . . . it was more than unsettling.

"I needed to assess the danger." She gave me a sad look then. One corner of her mouth curving down. "The monster is a clever beast. It hides in those you know. I needed to interact with them as you, so that I could see if it's already found you."

"And?" I prompted slowly, watching carefully. "Has it?"

"It's on your trail, but I don't believe it's infiltrated those close to you yet. It took out the witch you were talking to because she knew too much." Her eyes slid sideways once more, to where Shepard still wavered. "You should be careful interacting with ghosts too much. They work with the monster. Spy for it. You shouldn't trust anyone."

"Anyone but you?" I said. It was only a moment, but a flash of annoyance crossed her features as she realized how that sounded. The more my shock at seeing her wore off, the more I was coming back to my senses.

"Well—" she started, but I cut her off.

"You seem to know an awful lot about this monster, and yet it's me that's died multiple times." I put my hands on my hips, my suspicion mounting.

"I know a great deal because we're the ones that created it."

I blinked twice. Now that I was *not* expecting. Before I could gather my thoughts and come up with a response, Thana continued talking.

"We created it together and unleashed it upon the world. Something soured in it along the way. It wanted power for itself. So it turned on us. I wanted to put it down, but you thought you could save it." She smiled again, but it wasn't happy. It was almost pitying, but with a hint of warmth. "You always were soft."

I let out a snort of derisive amusement. "Yeah, right. Warm and fuzzy, I am not. Anyone who knows me will tell you I'm about the furthest thing from soft that you can be."

Thana studied me, her gray eyes cool and assessing. There was a detached calculation there that I didn't recognize. *Had I ever looked at anyone the way she's looking at me?* Instead of replying, she lifted her right shoulder in a bored shrug I definitely recognized. It was beyond creepy how her mannerisms were so like mine, and yet it was like meeting an alien. She possessed an otherness about her that I wasn't sure what to do with.

Was I supposed to trust her?

Hardly. I knew almost instantly that wasn't happening anytime soon. I'd lost too many people to trust someone that shared my face, showing up in town right after Darla was murdered. She claimed it was a monster, and her explanation sounded good. Almost a little too good, though.

She may be who she claimed, but something told me I didn't have the full picture.

And really—how could I? She claimed we'd been here since the beginning of time basically. There were a lot of questions to ask and a lot of ground to cover before she got anything resembling trust.

I glanced over my shoulder at Shep, wondering what he was thinking about this turn of events.

His body was tense, but his face was unreadable, giving nothing away. That, in itself, was telling. Shep didn't trust the bitch either. But was it because she was claiming his title, or for another reason?

Until I dealt with Thana and got Shep alone, it was clear I was not going to solve that riddle.

"As enlightening as this is, I was sort of in the middle of something with my actual twin, so how about you schedule something with my assistant, and we continue this conversation another time?"

There. That was subtle. Sort of.

Thana frowned, looking entirely too disappointed with me. "I know this isn't easy for you to believe after everything that's been happening around here, but you need to listen to me. You're in danger, and the only one who can keep you safe is me."

"I've been doing just fine on my own," I said, my voice hard this time.

That was a bit of a stretch. I'd died what, four times now? Five? Not a great track record . . . unless you considered the part where I came back each time more powerful than before. That was pretty cool.

The look in her eyes shifted then, almost like she'd decided to try a different tact with me because the whole 'your life is in danger' thing clearly wasn't working like she'd planned. "Salem," she said, reaching for my hand.

Energy tingled through me at the touch, and once again I stepped out of her reach.

Her expression turned mournful. "I have walked this realm alone for almost four centuries, searching for you. Trying to save you. Only to be too late every time. You are my sister. The only one who is my true equal. Don't you see? We need each other. It's the only way we can defeat this monster."

There was an earnest sincerity in her voice that had been lacking until now. I wasn't sure how to feel about it, but it was obvious to me that Thana truly believed what she was saying. Then again, James had believed in what he was doing too. Belief didn't make someone trustworthy.

"Look," I sighed. "I have a lot going on right now. This whole monster business is just icing on the cake—and while you may be my long-lost twin—I have a brother I'm trying to save, because he's the twin I know."

"I'm not asking you to run away with me. I know you too well to think that would ever happen. I just want to be a part of your life again," she said softly.

Indecision warred within me, but one thing was clear. This chick had answers. Answers about who and what I was. I couldn't completely blow her off. Not yet.

And really, I wasn't sure if I wanted to.

While I didn't trust her at all, I did get the distinct impression she felt attached to me. There was a kinship of sorts. It couldn't hurt to listen and see how this played out. I'd lost a lot of people lately . . .my eyes strayed to the spot where my father had been before he disappeared.

Maybe I could gain some too.

"I don't trust you," I told her.

Disappointment flashed through her expression as her lips pressed together and the corners of her eyes tightened. "I can't change that until you let me."

"I know." I crossed my arms over my chest as I regarded her. A pang went through me. Something I didn't understand, but I wanted to. "Here's the deal. I'm interested in staying alive instead of starting all over again. Teach me what we are, how to control my powers, and how to defeat the monster. I want to know everything—the good, the bad, and the ugly."

"That's not something you can learn overnight," she said.

"If it were, I'd be gravely disappointed in the universe for giving me something that easy for once," I replied in a bland tone.

She snorted, grinning over at me. "I suppose there is that," she said, coming closer once more. "You know, you have no memory of me. You don't know how much we've been through yet. Even after all this time, though, you're still the same."

"Don't be so sure," I said, pulling away. "We might have the same face. The same origin. A shared history. But I don't remember it. In this life, I am Salem. I had a twin brother, my best friend is a succubus, and my boyfriend is a reaper. You may have been around a while, pretending to be me—but you don't really know me."

"No," she said softly, stepping up beside me. "But I will."

My phone dinged in my pocket. I pulled it out and read the text from Graves.

"Where are you going?" she asked, following after me as I started walking toward the parking lot.

"The Council called a meeting. Every supernatural in Farrow's Square has to be there."

Cool fingers brushed my arm. I glanced over my shoulder.

"But you're not a supernatural," she said.

"Yeah, but they don't know that." I considered that for a moment as I resumed walking. "Well, most of them. The reapers have some inkling." Pausing, I called out, "Shep?"

He popped up in front of me. "Yeah?"

"Meet me at the morgue tonight. We're going to find you a body."

His gaze slid sideways, toward Thana. He clearly didn't trust her, but he kept those thoughts to himself for the moment as he nodded once, then disappeared.

"He doesn't care for me," she noted in a shrewd voice.

"You just barged in and claimed to be my long-lost twin from another life. He's skeptical," I said, making my way to the car once more. "Reasonably so."

Reaching the Impala, I flung the door open and hopped in. On the other side of me, Thana did the same.

"What are you doing?" I asked her.

"Coming with you," she answered like it was obvious.

"You can't come to a Council meeting."

"Why not?"

I put on my own pair of Ray-Bans and started the car up. "Because they don't know you, and they don't know what I am—and I'm trying to keep it that way."

She squinted at me. "Why?"

"Because"—I reached for words—"because they can't know."

"That's a dumb reason," she said.

"Hey! You're the one that just said a monster is hunting me," I argued.

"Yes," she agreed with an emphatic nod, her tone of voice sarcastic. "The supernaturals knowing what you are won't make a difference. The monster will find us in the end. It always does. In the meantime, I'd like to stay close to you. I know you don't trust me, but I want to make sure you're safe."

I put the car in reverse as I considered her words. The fact of the matter was, I didn't really want to let her out of my sight either, but I was pretty confident strolling into a Council meeting with a surprise twin from a past life was not going to do me any favors. I had more than enough on my plate without having to try and explain Thana's presence as well.

"How 'bout this," I said, eyeing her as the car started moving, "why don't you hang out with my aunt while I take care of reaper business? Then, when I get back, you and I can have that heart-to-heart."

I could see the desire to debate the point with me. It was written all over her face. It was a look I knew because I wore it all the time. It was the same battle that was constantly raging inside of me. The need to argue. To prove that my way was right.

I let out a little breath. Stubborn people were a real pain in the ass. This must be what Graves deals with whenever he's trying to convince me to just listen to him. The thought brought a small smile to my face, and I shook my head.

"Listen, I know you don't like this plan, but this is the way it needs to be. Regardless of your stance on the reapers, and supernaturals in general, things are . . .tenuous right now. Let's not throw the Daughter of Death grenade in the mix just yet, okay? Not until I've had a chance to wrap my head around it myself."

Thana fell quiet beside me, her arms crossed over her chest. "Fine," she agreed, blowing out a breath of her own.

Oh, Esme was going to love this. We only just got rid of one hostage for her to keep an eye on, and I was already bringing home a second. My eyes slid to Thana. Not that she knew that was the real reason for my suggestion. Let her believe whatever she wanted. Esme—and her trusty machete—would watch this girl like a hawk.

I sped down Mansion Lane, pulling up the drive to my house in less than five minutes. Graves was already waiting outside, his eyes widening slightly as he noticed the figure seated next to me in the Impala.

Killing the ignition, I popped out of the car. "Graves, there's someone I'd like you to meet."

His eyes narrowed on me. "I thought you said you were at the cemetery."

"I was."

Graves pressed his lips together and eyed Thana, who was out of the car and leaning against the passenger door. "This some kind of fucking joke?" he asked, looking between us.

I let out a humorless laugh. "Not unless the joke's on me. Graves, meet my," I paused to look at Thana, "what did you call yourself? My true twin?"

She eyed Graves shrewdly and gave a single nod.

The mistrust was evident in the hard lines of Graves' face. This introduction was going to get ugly fast if I didn't play this right. "Thana has been looking for me. She says she's here to help me deal with whatever's hunting me and to learn more about my powers. I'm going to have her keep Esme company until we get back from the Council meeting and have the chance to chat more."

While I was talking, I was staring hard at Graves, communicating with my eyes everything I couldn't say out loud. Trust me. Go with this. We can talk about everything when we're alone.

His expression was still hard, but he gave a slow nod.

"Your name is Thana?" he asked.

She lifted an eyebrow, her expression one of utter condescension. "She didn't stutter," Thana said.

Graves didn't wilt under her tone as he said, "Thana means death."

A cold smile curled around her lips. "I am a Daughter of Death. Just like Salem."

"Hm." He turned, angling his body away from her and toward me. "Can we talk?"

"On the way to the Council meeting. You said it was starting soon, and I don't think your dad will appreciate us being late," I said, moving past him. He grabbed my forearm, making me pause.

"Salem—"

"Later," I said softly, a promise in my voice.

Our eyes met, and his burned with questions. Heat stirred in my veins as his grip loosened, sliding down my arm as I stepped toward the door.

"Alright." He squeezed my hand once and let it go.

I flung the front door open. "Esme?"

I only had to call out once. Esme came around the corner wielding a scythe. She spun it around in a showy maneuver, but when her eyes fell on Thana, her grip slipped. The scythe slid sideways a foot before she regained her hold. Six inches of brown hair streaked with gray fell on the floor.

"Who's this?" she asked, holding the weapon in one hand as she strode forward.

"Thana. She's . . ." My words trailed as I struggled to find an adequate answer. While Esme had seen me do things other reapers couldn't do, we'd never gone into the differences—or the small fact that I was just another reincarnation of myself and had lived countless other lives before now.

"I'm Salem's twin," Thana said, taking it upon herself to speak. "Her true twin."

Esme narrowed her eyes, her thin lips pressing together. "I hate to break it to you, but I was there the day that girl was born." Esme pointed in my direction. "She came out with a brother, not a sister."

"In this life," Thana corrected. "In her original life, it was only her and I. You and her brother might be family to this reincarnation—"

I held my hand up for Thana to stop because she was not making this situation any better.

"Okay, look." I let out a sigh. "I wasn't completely upfront with you about *everything*. Right before we brought James back and told you I was a reaper, we learned that's not quite true. I'm what's called a Daughter of Death. No, I don't know what all that means yet. Thana here found me at the cemetery this morning, though, and she says we're sisters. Or we were."

Esme's eyes were bouncing between Thana and me, a small wrinkle deepening between her brows.

"We still are," Thana insisted like I wasn't speaking. I

shot her a pointed glare, and she gave me the same look right back.

"Anyways," I drawled, looking away from her. It was just too eerie. "There's a lot going on right now, and I have some explaining to do, but the Council just called a meeting, and Graves and I can't be late."

"Should I prepare the basement for our guest?" Esme asked with just enough of a smile it should have been disarming. I recognized the code, however. She wanted to know if Thana was a friend or an enemy. I wish I knew the answer.

"No . . . I don't think you guys need to be that formal. Maybe just hang out in the kitchen?"

Esme's eyes narrowed as she tried to suss out any hidden meaning in my words. I mean, I thought it was pretty obvious. The kitchen is where the knives were. If things went squirrely, Esme wouldn't be caught without a weapon.

Graves tapped his foot impatiently beside me. "Salem, we should really get a move on."

"Yeah, okay." My eyes darted between Thana and Esme one last time. "You two going to be okay?"

Thana gave me a wide smile. "I'm going to enjoy some time getting to know my new family."

Esme's expression was harder to translate, but the not-so-subtle shift of her grip on the scythe was unmistakable. "We'll be fine. You two run along. I'll just give Thana a tour of my machete collection."

Worry sat like a ball of lead in my stomach, but this really was my best option for the moment. I had to trust that Esme could take care of herself and pray that Thana's motives were as pure as she claimed.

"Alright, let's go," I said to Graves, turning back to the door.

He was already holding it open.

I'd barely put the car into drive when Graves was demanding answers.

"Spill it."

My eyes darted to the rearview, although I wasn't sure what I was expecting to see . . . we'd only been gone for about ten seconds.

"It's exactly like I said. She found me talking to Shep. Claims she's here to help. I didn't have enough time to interrogate her before you were blowing my phone up."

"A single text is hardly blowing you up."

I rolled my eyes. "It was the subtext of your text."

"Subtext?"

I nodded. "All broody and demanding."

"I don't brood."

"Sure you don't, cupcake—hey, speaking of. Are there any still stashed in the glovebox?"

Graves was shaking his head beside me. "You can't just change the subject because you're suddenly hungry."

"What?" I threw him a cheeky grin. "I worked up an appetite last night."

His blue eyes smoldered as they met mine, but he didn't give in. "Her timing is too convenient. After all those weird sightings of you . . . Salem, she looks identical."

"Well, duh. I mean . . . she's my fucking *twin*, Graves. As for the sightings, I know. Believe me, I haven't overlooked it, but I haven't gotten a chance to properly question her, but her story lined up with Darla's warning. I think she's telling the truth, Graves, but if she really is who she says she is, we have literally thousands of years to discuss it—and given how little we know about what I am, I wasn't passing up my only opportunity to learn. I couldn't let her come with, but I don't trust her enough to leave her alone. This way, we know where she is, and we can get answers as soon as we're done with the Council."

The muscle in his jaw flexed, but he gave me a terse nod. "I guess it's our only option for the moment."

"So, do I get that cupcake now?"

"Just drive, Salem," he said, sighing.

"I think I've more than earned it . . . I did just save every reaper, *and* I gave you at least three mind-blowing orgas—"

A plastic-wrapped treat smacked the side of my face.

I was too busy multitasking as I drove and unwrapped it, that I didn't even bother to complain that my new boyfriend had just pelted me in the face with my favorite snack. Sometimes a girl had to pick her battles, and somehow I had a feeling that there were some big ones on the horizon.

Dissension

THE COUNCIL ROOM WAS PACKED. People were pressed up against each other like cookies in a box. The air felt hot. Stifling, despite the air conditioner running on full blast. It wasn't just the number of people packed into the Council's meeting room, though. Tension settled over the crowd. It ran from one person to the next, growing heavier with each silent moment.

Graves and I shuffled into the back, trying not to be noticed given we were tardy.

The members of the Council sat, gathered around their long table. All except for Alexander, that was.

He stood apart from the others with his hands clasped behind his back.

"—the reapers have dealt with the problem. The Council has passed judgment that the werewolf in question will be given life on parole. He'll live with his pack, but be unable to leave their territory."

Looks like we were more than a little late if they'd already explained most of the situation, at least the version of it they were going by. I highly doubted Alexander was going to tell them all about his own son's involvement. Admitting that James had been a murderer and controlling the poor guy wasn't exactly a great way to instill faith in the reapers—or their leader.

"That doesn't sound very much like a punishment," a voice rose from the crowd, but I couldn't pick out where it came from.

One person was all it took to sow dissent among the mass of supernaturals. After everything that had happened, tensions weren't just running high. They were under incredible strain and threatening to snap entirely.

"He killed three vampires," another voice said, coming from the other side of the room.

The group right in front of Graves and I shifted uneasily.

"And two fae, let's not forget that," a third voice added, coming from the opposite side of the room. I pinpointed this one because she was standing near the front. Tall and ethereal, her lavender hair was tied to one side and her pale-yellow eyes were narrowed on the Council before us.

"I've given harder punishments in the bedroom," a fourth voice shouted. I recognized it as the Bettie Page look-a-like I'd met the first time I'd gone to Succubus United, also known as Sigma Upsilon. It was Laura, the dominatrix.

That one got a few chuckles from the crowd, but it did nothing to ease the growing unrest.

"That's hardly called for," Sarah Cunningham, Tamsin's mom, and the succubus/incubus representative on the Council said. Her voice was hard, but judging by the look on her face, I got the impression she didn't disagree.

"And you, Desdamona?" a distinctly masculine voice called. "You can stand for this injustice?" The man didn't yell or speak as loudly as the others. On the contrary, his voice was fairly soft. He stepped forward from the crowd of what I'd assumed was vampires given the distinct resemblance most of them had to both the vampire representative and Gretel, my ghostly Siri. His hair was dark, and skin unbelievably pale. There was a red glint to his brown eyes. A hardness of his features that reminded me of marble statues.

"There were special conditions and things in play that you do not know," the vampire representative replied, tapping her blood-red nails along the hard edge of the wooden table. Her expression was cold.

"Such as?" he asked.

"The Council decided they will not be disclosed," she replied, her voice quieter still.

I got the distinct impression that, like Tamsin's mom, the lady vamp didn't agree with the ruling. And if not even the Council could agree on the punishment, how did they expect the rest of the supernatural community to blindly accept it?

Graves and I exchanged uneasy looks as murmurs started to fill the room. The words themselves were indistinguishable, but the anger that laced them was unmistakable.

"This is bullshit," someone growled from the back, their anonymity making them bold.

A chorus of 'yeahs' sounded in agreement.

My eyes shifted back to the Council table, falling on the grizzled werewolf representative. Danger was coming off of him in waves. His eyes were narrowed, a soft red glow shining from the depths. His face was flushed, which only served to make the thick scar running down his face more noticeable. I didn't know the guy, but even I could tell he was barely reining in his temper.

"Serafina, how can you allow this?" the lavender-haired beauty questioned.

A woman with dark blue hair rose from her place at the table, her butterfly wings twitching with what I assumed was agitation. "Rules were broken, the Council does not disagree. But a vote was cast, and this is the path that was chosen."

"Notice how she emphasized it was the Council's choice?" I whispered to Graves.

He nodded. "The fae are rarely lenient. Anything less than execution would not appeal to them."

Despite the united front they were presenting, the Council was far from unified about this decision. Three of the seven must have fought against the choice. My gut was telling me that didn't bode well for the rest of us.

Alexander made an angry sound low in his throat. "Enough. The decision has been made. The Council's ruling is law. You will stop this foolish whining and return to your lives. Any further acts of violence against the wolf packs or the reapers will not be tolerated. We will enforce a zero-tolerance policy for anyone caught participating in such acts of hate. The threat is neutralized, the curfew is lifted, you are all safe. That is all you need to know."

Around us, the murmurs of dissent grew louder.

"Dirty soul-stealer," a low, angry voice hissed behind me.

"If there's a zero tolerance for violence, then why is the wolf-pup being shown leniency?" another voice cried out.

"Someone should tell your dad that ordering people to just get along rarely works out well," I whispered. "It's like telling someone to get over their feelings. Things aren't that easy. If anything, it's only going to make it worse."

Graves lifted a brow. "You think I don't know that?"

"So why is he acting like he's just done everybody a favor, then?" I asked, truly curious.

"Because he probably believes he did," Graves said.

I gestured to the crowd. "Is he blind? Do these people look happy to you?"

Graves' lips twisted in a grimace. "Some of them?" he replied, but it sounded like a question.

"Meeting adjourned—" Alexander started, but he was cut off by a dozen angry voices.

"You owe us justice, reaper!" a dark-haired vampire shouted.

"The dead have rights," another woman insisted.

Alexander's voice dropped to a scary, seething tone. "The next person who talks out against the Council's ruling will be imprisoned for the foreseeable future."

My eyebrows lifted. "I didn't realize stifling freedom of speech was a tenant of supernatural society."

"It isn't," Graves said, his voice hard. "He feels locked into a corner between the Council and his own position over the reapers. If people start questioning that position, there will be problems. He doesn't know how to fix the damage done, so he's falling back on the only thing he knows." Graves looked sideways, his blue eyes falling on me. "Aggression."

"If he actually imprisons someone for speaking out—" My own voice was drowned out as the vampire male from before interjected.

"The Council's ruling? Or *your* ruling?"

A hush fell over the room as Alexander's face turned red with anger.

"That's it." He snapped his fingers. "Dominick. Samuel. Dale—"

"Really, Desdamona? You'll stand for this? Your own kind silenced by a reaper who's gone soft?"

The man's open questioning of the vampiress told me things were only going to move from bad to worse if this kept up. Tempers were running high. The loss was too great. These people didn't want justice, they wanted revenge. Retribution.

Since James' role in the massacre—and his subsequent death—was being left out, these people didn't realize that the one at fault had already been dealt with. The werewolf —who was just sentenced to a lifetime of confinement within his packs' borders—was a victim of this same blind hate. His desire for vengeance after his brother was killed was what led him to kill James, who in turn split both his own soul and the wolf's. This all-consuming need for revenge was what started this mess, and if we didn't find a way to neutralize it—the bloody cycle would only continue.

"You were given a warning, Rembrandt, and you chose to not heed it. Regardless of your opinion on the ruling, you chose to speak." She lifted one pale shoulder, and the strap of her black slinky dress slid downwards as she watched in stone-cold silence while the three young reapers approached the vampire.

"This isn't right," I said under my breath.

"No," Graves agreed. "But it's the world we live in."

I frowned, not liking the complacency in his tone. Before I could say anything else, the lavender-haired fae stepped forward.

"This is wrong, Serafina. The wolf killed members of every species. He put the entire supernatural community at risk. This is a direct violation of the first rule, and the consequence has always been execution. The rules aren't being bent; they're being disregarded entirely. The reapers are supposed to uphold our laws. If they cannot fulfill their purpose in doing so, and the Council is choosing to cover it up instead of holding them accountable . . ." The fae woman trailed off and lifted a lavender eyebrow.

Serafina turned pale. "Don't you dare—"

"I invoke the Rite of the Masses on the grounds that the Council's ethics and judgment have been clouded by personal ties."

Silence filled the void where murmurs and cries of outrage had been only moments ago.

I turned to Graves, but his expression was locked down hard. "What does that mean?"

"We're going to vote," he said solemnly.

"On what?"

"On whether or not the Council members get to keep their positions."

"And if it's decided they don't?"

"Then we'll have to choose replacements, and they will reevaluate the werewolf's fate."

Rock the Vote

IF I THOUGHT the room was tense before, that was nothing compared to emotion overtaking the room now.

Excitement.

Outrage.

Violence.

They were all there, bubbling up like magma rising through the center of a volcano. Shit was about to erupt.

Alexander hadn't moved, but he was quietly seething from his place on the stage. Seraphina looked like she was about to faint. The other Council members were harder to read, but their expressions ranged from disinterest to curiosity to annoyance.

"Does this kind of thing happen all the time?" I asked Graves, wondering why people were so afraid of the Council if it was that easy to swap out members.

"Are you kidding?" Graves asked. "Who in their right mind wants to call out the Council in front of them? Even assuming that one of the three grounds allowing for Rite of the Masses has been met, can you begin to imagine what happens if the vote fails?"

"Isn't there, like, protection against retaliation or something?"

Graves gave me a look.

"I'll take that as a no," I muttered.

People began to shuffle around us, those that had been lucky enough to find seats rising to their feet as the lavender-haired faerie made her way to the stage.

"What are the grounds?" I whispered, as my eyes followed the fae's movements.

"Bias, corruption, and threat of reveal."

"Threat of reveal?" I repeated.

"Undertaking an act that would threaten to reveal our existence to the mortal world."

I pressed my lips together. They really did take rule number one seriously.

"What happens to a Council member that is voted out?" I asked, my voice dropping even lower.

"We don't stone them to death, if that's what you're asking."

"Well, I mean, you seem to want to execute people for everything else, so can you blame me for wondering?"

Graves shook his head, purposely fixing his eyes on the woman who was now standing just beside his father. The air of expectation swelled as Alexander cleared his throat.

"Nocturna, the floor is yours," he said, his voice smooth despite the slight tightening around his eyes.

Adjusting her leaf-colored dress, the lavender-haired fae woman stepped forward and stared out at the crowd, letting the silence and anticipation mount.

"Wait, we're doing this right now?" I hissed, eyes going wide.

"With something this big, it's better to act right away," Graves whispered.

"It seems a little extreme, having to vote right in front of them," I muttered.

"Thus my earlier comment," Graves said. "Now hush."

I scowled at him, my eyes drifting to the older-looking gentleman to my left. It was rare to see a supernatural with obvious signs of aging, especially with so many having extended lifetimes—reapers notwithstanding. He caught me staring, turning deep amber eyes upon me.

Sexual heat slammed into me, turning my core into a pool of molten liquid.

"Knock it off, incubus," Graves growled beside me, grabbing my arm and pulling me back.

I wasn't aware I'd tried to move closer to the stranger until the unexpected warmth faded and my head cleared.

"Jesus, that was intense," I muttered, blinking.

"Some of us get stronger with age," Graves said.

"No kidding," I murmured, moving a little closer to my reaper. So much had happened since returning home, sometimes I forgot how little I actually knew about the world I belonged to.

Finally, Nocturna started to speak. "People of Farrow's Square, the choice is up to you. The facts are before you. The Council has knowingly refused to act according to our most ancient laws—namely by not executing one who has proven themselves to be a significant and dangerous threat to the lives of our people, and a threat to exposing us all. In doing so, they fail to remain neutral, just, or fair. They have not acted in the best interest of all of Farrow's Square's citizens, but rather have allowed personal biases to inform their decisions. This betrayal of our laws cannot go unpunished. So I ask you now, remedy this failure. All in favor of removing the current Council members from their positions, raise your hand."

Hands flew up around us. There was no moment of indecision, no glancing around to see what others were doing. This was a decisive and determined choice, one that had clearly been made long before the faerie started speaking.

Graves and I were two of the only people not to lift our hands in the air. It wasn't hard to tell factions apart like this. The floor was at a bit of an angle, so even standing it was obvious who was—or wasn't—raising their hands. For the most part, the room seemed split by species. Not a single wolf had their hand up, while practically every vamp or fae did. The rest of us were more divided, but there was no doubt about the general consensus.

The vote passed.

The Council would be overturned.

Dread thickened in my stomach because I had a feeling that wasn't the only thing that would be overturned.

"What happens now?" I asked as the room broke out in a dull roar.

Graves grabbed my arm and dragged me out of the way of the exit as people started pushing their way toward it. "For the next twenty-four hours, the supernatural world has no Council."

"That doesn't sound very good," I commented as a group of vampires passed us, their dislike clear in their eyes.

"It's not. There's a lot of reasons the Rite of the Masses isn't called on often. The chaos that's going to ensue until a new Council is formed is one of them."

The last of the vamp crowd strode by, hissing at the werewolves that parted for them. A series of growls rumbled in the chests of a few good ol' boys that didn't take too kindly. I sensed a fight brewing when a voice rang out above them.

"Keep on walking. There's nothing to fight about. The vote has been cast, and that's the end of it." My best friend stood between two werewolves, her hands on her hips as she addressed the crowd. Unable to withstand her compulsion, the vampires walked out and the wolves turned away. The tension dissipated.

I pushed through the last of the crowd still lingering.

"It's a madhouse in here," I said as I approached her.

Tamsin turned and then paused. Leaning forward, she sniffed once. Her eyes blew wide. "You naughty girl—"

"Tam," I groaned, already knowing where this was going. "This is so not the place."

"As a succubus, I will have to respectfully disagree. Every place is a place to have sex with the right crowd," she grinned, and the werewolf beside her smiled back.

I ran a hand down my face. "Don't we have bigger things to worry about right now?"

"At least tell me it was worth it," she said, lowering her voice and leaning forward a fraction.

A grin worked its way up my face. "What do you think?"

She sniffed again, her eyes glowing brighter. "You went

back for seconds. He must be good. You usually taste and run."

My back prickled, and I sensed Graves standing behind me. The scent of spearmint and aftershave hit me. I gave Tamsin a look to shut up, and my best friend grinned. A mischievous glint entered her eye.

"She's 'addicted to my dick'. Isn't that what you told me, Salem?"

My face flamed.

"Oh look, there's your dad. I need to talk to him." I stumbled forward, making my grand escape but not before I heard both Graves and Tamsin laughing.

I glanced back to see her patting his shoulder. His eyes were still locked on my retreating form. A small smile curled around my lips as I approached the table. Alexander stood beside it, talking to Yasha and the ex-werewolf rep whose name I never learned.

"The witches and warlocks are unlikely to change our vote, even with a new head. We value balance and the sanctity of life. Particularly when the guilty party is not so guilty," Yasha said.

I slowed my steps, listening in.

"I wish I could say the same for the Brotherhood, but it's unlikely with a power shift. The reapers' vote is going to come down to who is selected," Alexander said.

Beside him, the werewolf looked up. His red-tinted gaze zeroed in on me. His voice was all snarl as he said, "Do you know what we do to eavesdroppers in my pack, little reaper?"

I should have felt bad, getting caught red-eared . . .as it

were. "Maybe you shouldn't talk about private things in a public setting, then," I replied.

Alexander's lips twitched. "Fair point, Ms. Shroud. As always."

The werewolf's lips pulled back and a low growl rumbled in his throat. Yasha placed her hand on his arm and shook her head. "We can continue this conversation later," she murmured.

The two of them walked away, and I turned back to Graves' dad. "It's Kaine," I reminded him.

Ignoring my correction, he said, "I'm sure you have many questions about the day's events, Salem—"

"Actually, you'd mentioned last night that you needed to speak with me."

He nodded, but it was distracted. "Yes, yes. I do, but now," he broke off and sighed. "I find myself a little busier than anticipated. Perhaps our conversation can wait another day or two? Just until things . . . settle down."

I raised a brow. His words said one thing, but the way he said them was sending an entirely different message. Alexander didn't believe for a second that things were going to settle.

"Can it? Are you sure it's . . .wise to hold off?" What I really wanted to ask was if it was safe to put off whatever it was he felt was so urgent for me to know, but if he was willing to delay enlightening me for the second time, perhaps what he had to share wasn't that important after all.

His lips tightened ever so slightly, but he gave me another nod. "To put it frankly, I don't have the time needed to fully have that discussion with you. We need to make our way to Gamma Rho. To vote." He smiled, but it was completely devoid of humor. His blue eyes were haunted and, dare I say, afraid.

Alexander had never seemed anything less than confident and in complete control. Even staring down James as he offered to kill his own son, he'd appeared outwardly calm. Seeing the change, albeit a subtle one, had unease slithering within me.

"Should I even be a part of the vote?" I asked.

Alexander blinked at me, confusion momentarily clouding his eyes. "What do you mean?"

"Well . . ." I dropped my voice. "It's not exactly like I'm a full-blooded reaper."

His expression cleared, but he matched my whispered tone. "No, but that is a fact best left to our house for the time being. As far as everyone else is concerned, you are a Grimm and your place is with us. Now if you'll excuse me, I should try and catch up with some of the others before the voting process begins."

Alexander was walking away before I could utter a goodbye.

"That didn't look like it went well," Graves said, coming up beside me.

I shrugged. "Wasn't much of a conversation. Your dad has a lot on his mind."

Graves snorted. "You think?"

"I overheard him saying that the new head of the reapers might vote in favor of execution," I said.

"And that surprises you?" Graves asked, turning his body so that we were concealed from anyone who might walk by.

"Well . . . yeah, I guess. I mean, they know the truth."

Graves lifted a brow. "A werewolf killed a reaper as retaliation for a sanctioned shredding. That's what kicked all this off, and no matter what else happened, that fact doesn't change. Add to it the part where that same wolf was at least partially responsible for the death of literally dozens of reapers over the last four years, it's hard to let that go. You aren't the only one who's lost family members, Salem. The whole thing is fucked, no matter how you look at it."

"I know. I'm the last person who should talk given how I kidnapped James and got a little stabby on occasion . . . I just don't want to lose anyone else. If this doesn't calm down, we're going to have an all-out supernatural war on our hands, and win or lose, people die in war. Not everyone gets to come back," I murmured.

I was thinking of Shep, and Tamsin, and Esme. I could save them. But what about everyone else? There came a point where even I had to have limits, surely? If the fighting became too obvious, the humans in Farrow's Square would figure it out. Some already had. Esme was proof of that. And what about the people I didn't get to? The ones I couldn't find and therefore couldn't save?

I shook my head. "We need to avoid a supernatural war like that at all costs."

His fingers skimmed my cheek, tucking a stray strand of pink hair back. "We will, and the way to do that right now is for us to vote on the best person to represent the reapers. We can't control anything else in this scenario, but we can contribute to that."

I nodded. He was right, but the feeling of dread didn't abate so easily. There was something coming, and it wasn't just the hunter searching for me and Thana. The tension between groups had reached its peak. After years of bitterness and bloodshed caused by James and Gerard, these people wanted revenge.

I wasn't sure if one execution would be enough to satiate them, though.

"Hey, Kaine! Graves! We gotta roll," Randy called out, loud enough to jar me from my own deep, and frankly depressing, thoughts.

"We'll be right there," Graves said.

Randy shrugged, and the last of the room emptied as the reapers left.

"Come on," I sighed, heading for the door. "I need to check in on Esme and Thana before we head over. I wasn't planning to leave them alone for so long."

Graves dropped a hand on my lower back as we stepped out of town hall. The parking lot was still littered with supernaturals. Several eyes turned to us as we descended the steps, and his hand shifted to curl around my hip, pulling me into his side.

I angled my head, lifting an eyebrow.

"Trying to make a statement, Graves?" I asked lightly.

"Something like that," he muttered, guiding us toward the Impala.

My heart tightened in my chest, but I didn't say anything as we climbed in. I turned the key in the ignition and the engine roared to life. The couple of supes that were lingering near the car jumped away as I put us into reverse and whipped out of the lot. It didn't miss my attention that Graves' hand went to the oh-shit bar.

"Trying to make a statement, Salem?" he parroted back to me.

"Something like that." I grinned.

As soon as we hit the highway, I pulled out my cell and dialed Esme. The sound of a chainsaw in the background was the first thing that greeted me.

"Everything alright?" Esme's voice filtered through.

"Shouldn't I be the one asking you that?" I replied, merging into the left lane before gunning it.

"Everything's fine here," she said, sounding decidedly distracted.

I narrowed my eyes. "Then why do I hear a chainsaw in the background?"

"Oh, that? We're making art."

"Art?" I replied skeptically.

"Mhmm," my aunt hummed, still distracted.

"Esme, if something's up, you should tell me—"

"Everything's all good, Salem. We'll see you when you get home. Bye!" The line went dead, and the urge to bang my head on the steering wheel was great.

"Should we stop by your place?" Graves asked.

"No." I blew out a frustrated breath. "Esme's acting weird, but that's not out of character for her. I'm more worried I'm going to come back to find half my house demolished than anything else. Let's get this vote over with so I can figure out what the fuck those two are up to."

And the Winner is

GAMMA RHO WAS PACKED by the time we got there. Graves and I ended up having to park a few blocks away and walk back. As we approached the front of the house, the cacophony of voices greeted us.

Since we were some of the last to arrive, Graves and I were stuck standing in the back of the room.

"Does it look like anyone is missing?" a familiar voice called.

I had to stand on my tip-toes to make out Dom's head over the guy in front of me.

Reapers looked side to side as they tried to figure out who might not be present. After a minute, it seemed that anyone who was supposed to be here was.

"Alright," Dom said, continuing to take charge of this impromptu meeting. "I know that a lot of us probably have questions about what went down tonight. It's been a long time since we've had to do one of these, so I'm going to go over the rules to make sure everyone understands what's at stake."

Given the number of people present, you would think there would be lots of ambient sound, but the room was dead silent. If not for the tickle of hair against my neck, I wouldn't be certain people were actually breathing right now.

"We have twenty-four hours to vote for a new rep. No one leaves until that rep is decided, so let's not waste time fucking around debating useless issues. I don't think I need to remind any of you how important this decision is. Not only will this person be the head of our house, they will also be the deciding factor in any issue brought before the Council as a whole in the case of a tie. We cannot afford to let petty bullshit interfere with making the right choice. That said, we will start by opening up the floor for nominations. You cannot nominate yourself, and if nominated, you cannot decline. Once all nominations have been cast, we will start the voting process. Any questions?"

Off to the side of the room, Alexander stood, arms crossed and watching. While he wasn't crazy about losing his spot on the Council, he was at least enough in his right mind to try to help us move forward as well as we could. I'd give him that.

When no one answered, the nominations began.

"I nominate Morte Senior," one of the older reapers said. He had a gruffness about him that reminded me of the way my dad talked about my grandad.

An older reaper with brown hair streaked gray and hard brown eyes stood. He was tall with proud shoulders that didn't sag despite the burdens that marred the lines of his face. Four scars ran from his cheek to jaw. It didn't take a genius to guess a werewolf had done it.

He'd gotten lucky he hadn't taken that full blow to the head or he wouldn't be here.

"I nominate Dominick Soul," Alexander said.

Dom looked at the ex-representative and nodded once. I glanced at Graves, wondering if he was hurt that his father hadn't picked him, but his expression was unreadable.

A few more names were called, and those reapers also stood. I could tell we were nearing the end of the line here.

"Anyone else?" Dom called. The group rustled, but no one spoke up. "Alright, if that's all—"

"I nominate Salem Kaine," Randy said.

My jaw dropped open. No one, and I do mean no one, was more surprised than I was.

"I—you can't do that," I said.

"You can't decline," Dom said.

I narrowed my eyes at Randy. He meant well, I'm sure. Randy always did.

That didn't change that it was a fucking stupid decision.

"I'm not a true reaper, so he can't nominate me," I replied.

"You're close enough," Dom said with a shrug.

"I'm really not." My feet edged toward the door, and Graves' arm tightened around my waist. I flashed him a cold look, and he returned it.

Asshole.

"Does anyone here have an issue with Salem being nominated?" Dom asked the room.

Silence met his question.

There was a time I wanted this. To be accepted. If not

appreciated, then at least be seen as one of them. Now, though . . . there was too much shit going on. I had Thana to deal with. I had my own powers to sort out. Not to mention the monster hunting me.

Putting me on the Council would be a terrible decision, most of all because I lacked the thing you needed most as a leader: tact.

"Alright, then," Dom clapped his hands together. "Time to vote."

And so the process began.

Each name Dom called out, every brother had to vote, starting with mine.

"Salem Kaine," he said, respecting my last name as Randy had, instead of referring to me as a Shroud the way Alexander did.

I was surprised when fourteen hands went up in the air. Glancing sideways, I noticed with relief that Graves wasn't one of them.

"You'd make a terrible Council member," he said with a shrug. Completely unapologetic.

I couldn't agree more. Too bad that many of the reapers in the actual frat didn't agree.

It appears that saving their lives made them think I was fit to lead.

They should have realized the only thing that made me fit for was bragging rights about bringing them all back from the dead.

Thankfully, fourteen wasn't enough to keep me in the running. Two of the nominees, Morte Sr. and Dom, tied with nineteen votes.

"What happens now?" I whispered to Graves.

"Now we vote again, until a majority is found."

I frowned, really hoping this wouldn't stretch on much longer. Meetings were about as exciting as watching paint dry as far as I was concerned. Maybe less. There were about one hundred things I would rather be doing—even leg day was starting to look appealing—although this vote technically was one of the most important things I'd been a part of in the last couple months. At least as far as the reapers were concerned. Well, that and saving their asses. They probably appreciated that.

Silence took over the room once more and then Dom said, "All in favor of Tenison Morte to become the next Council member?"

I mentally tallied the number of hands that lifted. Twenty-one. Dom was going to win this shindig.

Judging by his expression, Dom hadn't expected that either. Looking stunned, he said, "All in favor of—"

I raised my hand with over half the room. Dom might be a Fuckface, but after working with him to hunt the werewolf, he'd grown on me. Somewhat. Not that I was going to tell him that.

I thought he was open-minded enough to at least try to be fair, given how he handled my short time being locked up by the Brotherhood.

Alexander pushed away from the wall, a grim sort of smile on his face. "And so it's decided. Dominick Soul, you are the new head of the Grimm Brotherhood. Congratulations."

Dom's eyes went wide. "Thank you, sir."

"Why don't you and I head upstairs? There are some

matters I should bring you up to speed on before your first official meeting tomorrow."

Dom nodded and then glanced back at the rest of us. "Uh . . . meeting dismissed for now."

There were a few cheers and a scattering of applause as everyone vacated the room.

I glanced back at Graves. "Better him than me."

"Definitely," he agreed with a grin. "Pretty sure your being in charge is a precursor to the end of the world."

I punched him in the arm. "Ha ha," I said dryly. "I didn't see you fighting for the chance to sit on your ass and make decisions that impact everyone else."

"I think I've got my hands full as it is," he said, his eyes searing me as his lips curled up in a smile.

Tingles skittered down my spine. "Speaking of . . . do you think we could head up to your room for a bit? I want to try something."

His eyebrow lifted. "Try something?" he repeated, leaning closer.

Goosebumps broke out over my arms, but I wasn't cold.

As suddenly as he'd crowded my space, he stepped away and motioned for me to go first. I turned, feeling his eyes on me as I walked up the stairs and stopped at his door.

I twisted the knob and stepped inside. The door closed behind me.

"What's this about?" Graves asked, crossing his arms over his chest.

Instead of responding to him, I called out softly. "Darla."

I waited a moment. Then two. Frowning when nothing happened. I repeated her name again and still nothing.

On the third attempt, it was more of a growl than anything. When no puff of smoke or eerie ghost appeared, I hung my head.

"Why are you calling Darla?" Graves asked, moving in front of me to lean back against his desk.

"Thana was there the night she died. She said it was the monster that's been hunting me. I wanted to try to speak to Darla without her around," I explained.

"Because you think Thana's lying?"

"Because it's too fucking convenient." I ran a hand through my shaggy pink hair. "I . . . I think there's a lot going on, and I don't have all the pieces. Thana claims she can help. She says she wants to protect me. After everything that's happened, though, you can understand why I don't want to go on just her word alone."

Graves tilted his head forward in a nod. "I would be seriously questioning you right now if you did. Tell me about this monster."

I repeated back to him everything Thana told me earlier. By the end, a frown marred his full lips.

"She seems sincere in missing me. It's the other stuff that I question."

"I don't like it," Graves said. "But if she is who she claims she is, I have a feeling she's not going to give up on you very easily."

"Yeah, I don't think so either. I figure in the meantime, while this Council shit is going on, we keep her under wraps. If people realize I have a long-lost twin who has no qualms about telling them what we really are . . . I can't imagine it going well. Thana doesn't seem to give a shit what anyone thinks."

"If we're going to keep her away from the Council, you and Esme are going to have to entertain her a lot of the time. Use it to your advantage. Make her train you and learn more about this monster."

"That's the plan," I said. "But I need you to play nice with her in the meantime."

"You're questioning *my* ability to 'play nice'?" He tilted his head, amusement dancing in his eyes.

"You tend to be a jackass when you don't trust people," I said bluntly.

"Because most people aren't worthy of that trust," he replied in the same tone.

"She wants to try to earn it, Graves. And while I'm not jumping headfirst here—I want to give her a chance."

His eyes bore into me. "So give her a chance, Salem. But promise me one thing."

"What?"

He leaned forward, grabbing my hand and using it to pull me into him. I stood between his legs. "That you won't leave town. No matter what she says."

I blinked, my head whipping back. "I have no intention of leaving town anytime soon. Not that I could, anyway. The Council wouldn't be happy with me."

"I'm just making sure," he said softly. "You don't get to run from me, and you sure as shit don't get to leave because she convinces you it's for your safety or some other bullshit I feel like she's going to pull."

I pressed my lips together, my heart beating fast. "I'm not leaving."

"Good." He leaned forward, his lips brushing against mine. It was tentative at first, more questioning than claiming.

I opened my mouth, letting my tongue twine with his. A groan escaped him. I fisted both hands in his hair, pulling him closer. Strong arms wrapped around my waist.

"We shouldn't do this here," he said against my lips.

"Are you sure about that?" I asked in a husky tone. "We could be fast . . ."

"Seriously, Salem?" a voice demanded from behind me.

I froze, and Graves did the same.

"You've got to be kidding me," I muttered.

"You *just* fucked him."

I open and closed my mouth, at a loss for words.

Shep didn't wait for a reply. "I thought we had a date with my new body tonight. When you didn't show, I got worried, so I came to check on you. Imagine my surprise to find you playing tonsil hockey with my best friend." He sighed. "I've been dead for a while now. I wanna get back to my life, Sis. Time's a ticking."

I groaned, and this time it had nothing to do with pleasure.

"Ghost?" Graves asked.

"My brother, to be exact."

Graves' hands dropped away from me, and Shepard made a sound of disgust.

I let out a chuckle. "Little late for that one, Graves. Apparently, Aurora was watching us last night and decided to fill them all in."

Graves, badass super-reaper, blushed. "Uh, sorry you

had to find out that way," he managed, knowing Shep would hear him.

Shep rolled his eyes, but he was smiling. "Tell him not to get his panties in a bunch. I don't actually care. You could do a lot worse," he added, looking at me.

I glared at him, but repeated his words for Graves' benefit. Then I said, "Shep, I don't think we can go to the morgue tonight. There's been a bit of a situation here."

"Morgue?" Graves asked, his brows dropping low.

"I'm going to help Shep find a new body."

"Uh, Salem, allow me to point out the obvious," he started.

"He better not be body blocking me," Shepard muttered, crossing his arms and giving Graves a hard stare.

"You can't just reanimate a dead body," Graves continued, causing Shep to throw his hands up in exasperation.

"Of course I can . . . no one else is using it. What's the harm?"

"Don't you think people are going to notice that someone who was officially found dead is suddenly up and walking around?" Graves pointed out.

My expression dropped at the exact same time as Shep's. No, I hadn't thought about that at all.

Graves sighed with exasperation. "What you should do, if you're dead set on this, is wait around the hospital. People have near misses on the tables there all the time. Should be easy enough to slip Shep into someone within less than a minute of the original owner taking off. That'll raise less eyebrows at least. Although," he added, frowning again, "it could get sticky if the person has family present. Or living family at all."

"So what you're saying is we have to find a unicorn? Someone no one else will miss, like John Doe or something, in addition to just happening to be present at the exact moment they die so we can make the swap without people noticing. Super. Should be a cake walk," I said dryly.

Shep's expression matched mine. "Definitely not something you'll be able to knock out in twenty minutes."

"Nope," I sighed. "Sorry, Shep. This is going to take a bit more time and planning than I can manage right now. I need to get back to Esme and Thana." At his crestfallen expression, I added, "We'll figure it out though, I promise."

My twin fought to hide his disappointment, but I always could see right through him. "It's all good, Sis. I get it. What's a few more days?"

"I'm really sorry—"

Shepard waved away my apology. "Don't worry about it. Speaking of the fake twin. You need to be careful with Thana, Salem."

"Careful? Why?"

His expression was determined, but also guarded. Like he was about to say something he knew he shouldn't. "She's—"

But that was all he managed before Graves' door burst open, swinging through my twin's ghostly form and interrupting whatever it was he was trying to say. I scanned the area, checking to see where he went, but Shep was gone. Damnit, I really needed to talk to him about this whole Thana thing.

"There you are," Tamsin said, her expression wild.

"Tam? What the hell are you doing here?" I asked,

shock and concern fighting for dominance as I reached for her.

"Guess who just got named head bitch in charge?"

I shook my head, not familiar enough with the succubi or incubi to make an educated guess.

"This bitch."

Tiebreaker

"*You're* in charge of SU now?" Graves asked, completely incredulous. I elbowed him in the ribs.

"As well as the rest of my kind," Tam said coolly with a saccharine smile.

"And I'm in charge of ours," a voice behind her said. I glanced past her shoulder to see Dom standing there with his arms over his chest.

"Really?" she asked with a cringe. "Man. The reaper pickings must not be great if you lot picked—"

"You need to leave," Dom said, cutting her off.

"What?" Both Tam and I said at the same time.

"I'm not going to ask again, so from one Council member to another—congratulations, but get out." He thrust his chin toward the stairs, and Tamsin pressed her lips together.

"Alright, Reaper. I see how it is." She leaned forward and kissed my cheek, whispering not too quietly, "Let me know when you remove the stick from his ass."

I snorted.

Dom's expression didn't change as she sauntered down the hall.

"What was that for?" I demanded.

He waited to answer until the front door closed loudly downstairs, signaling her exit. "Your protection."

I blinked, taken aback. "Uhhhh . . . you do realize I can't die, right?"

Dom sighed, shaking his head. "I don't know how you deal with her," he said to Graves.

"Bribes," he answered without hesitation.

I swatted him in the chest.

"Anyways, that's exactly what I'm talking about. I'm putting a no-guest policy down for the foreseeable future. The rest of the Council doesn't know what you are, and with how high tensions are running, we don't want them to think we have what amounts to a super soldier. You need to keep your powers under wraps. I'm going to talk to the guys and make it clear not one of them is to say a word to anyone. Unless absolutely mandatory, stay off campus if you're not here, and stay away from other supernaturals."

I opened and closed my mouth, not sure how to respond. For one, I was basically back to where I started when I came to town: in hiding.

However, Dom had a good reason. Fucker.

Of course I voted for him, and this is what I get. But . . . there was one good thing that would come of it.

I would get plenty of time to deal with Thana.

"I'll try to keep a low profile for now," I said.

His eyebrows drew together. "Really? You will?"

I narrowed my eyes. "Have I ever lied to you, Fuckface?"

His look of surprise morphed into annoyance. "I'm

your superior now. You're going to have to stop insulting me."

I let out a laugh at that, wiping the corners of my eyes. "Am I? Did I treat Alexander any better when he was in charge?"

"No, but—"

"Do you want me to stay away?" I asked testily.

Dom bit down whatever his following response was. "Yes," he answered through gritted teeth.

"Then I'll call you whatever I want. Not like you can do anything about it. As you said yourself, I'm basically a super soldier. One that currently feels like listening."

Graves let out a chuckle as Dom massaged his temples.

"Just . . . get out of here. Both of you. I've got other shit to deal with right now." He turned on his heel and walked away, not looking back once or he would have seen the grin on my face.

"I'm half convinced you voted for him just to fuck with him," Graves said as we stepped out of his room.

"Nah, that's just a bonus."

We were still chuckling as we walked through the frat house and back to the car.

"Man . . . Tam and Dom in charge. That's going to be entertaining," I murmured as we took off.

"No kidding. It'll be interesting to see who the others choose."

"I'd put money on that lavender-haired chick. She seemed to have a lot of sway, what with calling for the vote in the first place."

Graves nodded beside me. "Yeah, I think Nocturna is a given. The others? Anyone's guess."

"Well, we'll find out soon enough."

We fell silent after that, each of us lost to our thoughts as we pondered what fresh hell these new changes would bring because there was no way things would be smooth sailing. Changes of this magnitude always had ripples. I was willing to bet this time the ripples would be a damn tidal wave.

I swung off Mansion Lane and into the drive, eyeing my house warily.

"Why are you looking at it like it's going to grow legs and run at us?" Graves asked with a smirk.

"Because with the way my life has been lately, that's exactly what will happen."

Graves squeezed my knee. "I think you're probably safe. At least until we walk through the door."

"Expecting a crossbow?" I asked, shooting him a grin as we walked up to the door.

"I think I might be disappointed if she doesn't shoot at us. Means she doesn't see us as a threat," Graves murmured as I pushed the door open.

"To be fair, I don't think Esme sees anyone as a threat."

Other than his footsteps and soft chuckle, the house was silent. My stomach twisted.

"Uh oh," I whispered, setting my keys on the table and moving deeper into the house. "That can't be a good sign. Esme? Thana?"

When I finally found them, my mouth fell open in shock. I couldn't manage to find the words to announce my presence as I gaped at them, Graves in a similar state at my back.

Thana and Esme were on the floor, bodies contorted as they both tried to reach for a green circle with their feet.

Here I was, more than half expecting them to be in the middle of a mutual assassination, and they were busy playing a friendly game of Twister. Okay, maybe not friendly. There was a decidedly competitive gleam in both their eyes, but out of all possible scenarios that had flitted through my mind, this one hadn't been one of them.

"Uh, hey guys," I finally managed.

"Hi dear," Aunt Esme panted, not bothering to look up as she nudged the spinner with her finger. "Right hand blue," she called out.

I watched in rapt fascination as my aunt and my doppelgänger barely managed to maneuver into place.

"Having fun?" Graves asked.

Thana glanced at us over her shoulder, her ass high in the air.

"You better keep your eyes on her face," I gritted out in a low voice. "Don't care if her body looks like mine."

Graves brushed his hand against my lower back, and I felt his lips graze my neck. "Green isn't your color, Salem."

I grunted.

"This is our tie breaker," Thana announced, totally unaware of the conversation taking place between us. Or at least acting like it. "Esme kicked my ass at darts, and then I trounced her at rock climbing, so we're seeing who the winner is."

I frowned. "Darts and rock climbing, huh?"

"Nothing wrong with a little test of skills," Esme said, her face red but determined.

"How exactly are those a test of skills?" I asked.

"I thought it was fairly obvious. One for accuracy, the other strength," Thana informed me, her focus back on their game. "Both heavily mixed with strategy. Twister also includes endurance, flexibility, and mental stamina."

"If you say so," I said, shaking my head and adding to Graves, "I can't with these two."

"It's better than the alternative," Graves murmured back.

"That being . . ." I trailed off. The look in his eyes told me exactly what he meant.

The alternative of Esme being dead. Again.

I swallowed hard.

"I'm going to get some food. You guys come find me when you're done—"

"Left foot red," Esme grunted.

In the next second, Thana's eyes glinted deviously as her foot swept out and knocked Esme off balance. My aunt hit the ground with a thump, and my gray-haired twin contorted her body into place. She held the pose for a few seconds as Esme lashed out and tried to do the same. Thana was far faster. In a flash, her body whipped around in a show of both flexibility and strength that I certainly did not have.

It occurred to me that Thana was probably entertaining Esme. Then again, knowing my aunt, she was probably doing the same.

Her gray eyes met my own. "I'll join you," she said, suddenly standing up like none of this had happened.

Esme let out a curse. "This isn't over," my aunt called.

"I'd expect nothing less of a reaper," Thana replied. I paused, looking between my aunt and my doppelgänger.

"Esme isn't a reaper."

"Yes, she is," Thana said, strolling past me and toward the kitchen. "She's too fast or strong to be human, and she comes from a reaper line. Although"—she glanced back at my aunt as if assessing—"you look older. Reaper lifespans are longer. How long ago did you die?"

Esme, not missing a beat, answered, "Week or so."

Thana nodded. "That makes sense. The aging has slowed, but it's not reductive."

"Wait," Graves said. "So, women can be reapers?"

"Of course. It's only the Brotherhood's own misogyny that keeps your faction smaller, and therefore, weaker." Thana strode by, tossing the words over her shoulder almost flippantly.

"You've only been in town for all of what? A week? How do you know this?" Graves asked.

Thana's eyes flashed. "I see you've caught this one up to speed."

"Answer the question," Graves replied, his voice hard.

Thana let out an exaggerated sigh. "I'm over four hundred years old. Do you seriously think I only *just* discovered the reapers? Come now. I thought you were smart. Salem's past selves usually picked more intelligent partners."

Graves' fist clenched, and I stepped between them.

"You seem to know an awful lot about her past selves," Graves said.

Thana narrowed her eyes. "I always search for her. Sometimes I was lucky, and I got there soon enough. Other times . . ." Something flashed in her gaze that almost looked like regret. "I was too late."

"And yet she died every time, all the same. Makes me wonder how well you can truly protect her from anything," Graves said almost nonchalantly. His words were anything but.

Thana's expression darkened. She stepped forward, the front of her body only an inch from mine, but it wasn't me she was looking at.

"You might be faster and stronger than a human, but I created you, *mortal.* You are nothing but a weak, watered-down version of us."

Her chilled words cut me to the core.

I opened my mouth to correct her, but Graves' hand settled on my shoulder.

"If I am so weak by comparison, perhaps you should show me just how superior you are?" he said softly.

My eyes narrowed on my twin. While I knew what he was doing, I didn't like them arguing like this. Call it jealousy. Call it territorial. I didn't really care, but Graves was mine to argue with until we both pissed each other off enough we needed to make out. I didn't like seeing that same tension building between them.

"I hate to break up this little threesome you kids got going—"

"Esme!" I snapped.

My aunt lifted both her hands. "No judgement, Salem. I've participated in my own share of sexual experiments."

I was going to be sick. The urge to act like a child and stuff my fingers in my ears while saying "la, la, la" was great. I chose to be an adult and settle for crossing my arms over my chest, putting a little more of a buffer between Graves and Thana.

"Do you have a point you were working toward?" I asked.

"Yes, actually." She pointed across the room. "Who are they?"

I glanced over and did a double take. "Gretel? Rumpy? What are you guys doing here—" My words dried up on my tongue. They weren't translucent like they usually were.

They were . . . real.

"Hello, Salem," Gretel said, all business. She looked past me. Her eyes hardening. "Thana."

My sister's lip curled back in a snarl.

It hit me at once, the realization of who and what I was staring at, but that didn't make sense.

The ghosts had been here since the beginning. Even if they were spying, Thana said the monster hadn't found me . . .

Unless that wasn't true. She just hadn't found *it*.

When the Dead Come Calling

"WHAT THE FUCK, NOT-MORTICIA?" I said, slipping into my old nickname for the tween vampiress. "You can" —I gestured at her body—"turn yourself into a real girl and you're only just now making use of it?"

I wasn't ready to accept that Gretel was here for nefarious purposes, even though she was shooting definite eye daggers at Thana right now. The ghost girl had been with me since the beginning, and while she was an annoying shit most days, she hadn't let me down yet. I could give her the benefit of the doubt a little while longer.

Gretel gave me a long, bored look. "I'm here to deliver a warning."

"A warning? For who?" I asked.

Her ancient eyes swept across all of us, but landed on me. "You have one week to eliminate the abomination, or we will come back and do it for you. Trust me when I tell you, you do not want that to happen. If we have to take matters into our own hands, there will be no survivors."

Gretel started to blur at the edges, and not knowing what else to do, I lunged toward her.

Thana was faster. She was across the room standing in front of the very corporeal ghost, with her hand around her throat before I managed to lift my leg.

"Who sent you?" she snarled.

"You know," Gretel replied, her voice as even and cold as always.

If Thana had a reaction to that reply, I couldn't see it with her back facing me.

"What abomination?" I shouted, desperate for more information, but certain that I wasn't going to get it.

"Now's not the time to play stupid, Salem. You have a week."

Thana's free hand was plunging into Gretel's chest, but the almost teenager grinned, a savage look that had chills racing down my back, and she vanished. There wasn't even a puff of smoke this time. She was just . . . gone.

"What the fuck just happened?" Graves demanded.

But there wasn't time to answer him.

The walls began to shake, books and dishes flying off shelves, furniture toppling over. I may not be a native Californian, but I recognized an earthquake when I felt one. Although, the ground wasn't so much shaking as the house itself.

"Get to a doorway!" I shouted, not that I was sure it would be much of a help when things seemed to be flying across the room.

Esme was the first to act, grabbing Thana by the wrist and tugging her along. Graves and I were moving in the opposite direction. Before we even managed to reach the other doorway, the sound of hundreds of ghostly voices began to wail.

I'm not talking about a bunch of sad sack ghosts crying about their plights. I'm talking front row at a metal concert, sirens screaming, literal blood was coming out of our ears, wailing. My brain rattled around in my head, the noise so painful that tears were leaking from my eyes, and I dropped to my knees.

I couldn't think, let alone stand.

My eyes were squeezed shut, so I couldn't tell if the others were faring any better. I couldn't hear any screams, but that didn't mean anything, because I couldn't hear *anything* over that ghostly shriek.

Then, as quickly as it began, the noise faded.

The resulting silence was disorienting. Ringing filled my ears and I couldn't hear anything at all. It was like stepping into an old movie.

People were moving. Talking. I could see their actions, but the words didn't filter through.

My entire head felt like it was going to explode, the residual pain still so intense it rendered me speechless.

Despite that, though, it wasn't the pain that preoccupied my thoughts.

Across the room from me, Thana lifted her head. Our gray eyes met. Blood dripped from her ears as well, but there was a dangerous sort of detachment in her expression, like the pain didn't even register. Rage burned in her eyes.

I moved my mouth, trying to form words, but the act proved too difficult.

The ringing had abated, but my pain tolerance was only so high.

Hands gripped my waist as darkness started to close in and, despite my desire to do otherwise, I drifted.

SOMETHING WARM BRUSHED against my cheek. I leaned into it. A groan escaped me as that warmth trailed down my neck, over my shoulder, and down my back. I hummed in approval.

A masculine chuckle pulled at my attention.

I rolled, and that warmth clamped around my hip. Reaching out, I ran my hand down his side. My fingers seemed to have a mind of their own as they slid into his waistband.

"Best not to do that when your aunt is only a few rooms down."

My eyes snapped open. If not for the complete darkness of my dreams, I wouldn't have been able to make out the dark shapes of my bed and dresser and door.

We were in my room.

The tightness in my chest eased. I released a breath. I turned my head and groaned; my neck popped.

"Motherfucker," I muttered. "Why am I so stiff . . ." It came back to me then. The day before. Going to the grave-yard. Thana. The Council. The ghosts.

I winced at the phantom memory of my eardrums bursting.

"The ghosts bombarded you and Thana. You took it the worst because her body healed as the damage was being done. It seems you're not quite far enough in your level-ups for that to happen."

I rolled onto my back, feeling every hard ridge of him pressed up against me.

When I'd passed out from the pain, waking up in bed with Graves was not where I thought that would go.

"Where is she?" I croaked.

Warm fingers skimmed my side lazily.

"Sleeping in Shep's room. She wanted to stay with you, but I wasn't leaving, and apparently Esme has decided she'd rather leave you in my hands than your long-lost sister's." A smirk tugged at his lips.

"I need to talk to her. I've never seen ghosts just become real like that. And their warning—"

"Thana has a lot of explaining to do. She said she wasn't saying shit until you woke up, though."

"Did she actually say it like that?"

Graves laughed. "Yes. She seems to flip in and out of speaking like she's as old as she claims."

"It's weird," I said, my thoughts drifting.

"Very weird." He agreed. "How are you feeling?"

"Wait," I said, pushing myself up so I could look at him. "How are *you* feeling?"

Graves scratched the back of his head, the move causing his shirt to lift. If I wasn't so focused on hearing his answer, I definitely would have been distracted by the flash of that mouthwatering vee. "I feel about as good as you do, probably, thanks to Dom and the fucking blood rite. The ghosts screaming was hard on me, but not as bad as you. Your eardrums both burst under pressure."

"But if my eardrums burst, then how are you—"

"Fine?" He chuckled. "I wasn't. I just have a higher pain tolerance than you, and I was more motivated in putting a buffer between you and that bloodthirsty sister of yours. I don't want her knowing about the blood rite just yet, which means one of us had to stay awake. We've been healing over the last few hours. Thankfully, reaper hearing isn't as sensitive, and Esme is pretty much fine apart from a bad headache."

"So Esme's fine now?" I asked.

"Same as ever. If anything, she seemed excited about the idea of facing off with a pack of ghosts."

"Of course she did," I said with a sigh. Everything in me wanted to lay back down and use Graves as a human body pillow, but with the memory of the day before came the memory of Gretel's threat. She may call it a warning, but that didn't change the truth.

Gretel had given me a deadline. I'd already lost valuable time sleeping, and the only person who could help me figure out what was going on was the girl in the room across the hall.

"Hey, where are you going?" Graves asked as I swung my legs over the side of the bed.

I stood with a low groan, my body cracking and popping as I stretched my arms over my head. "Duty calls," I said, looking back over my shoulder at him.

I shouldn't have done it. He was even more tempting than usual, all splayed out on my bed with his hair rumpled with sleep, wearing the sweats he'd borrowed from Shep riding low on his hips.

"Fuck my life," I groaned, pressing the heels of my hands to my eyes. Now that I knew just how good it was between us, it was almost impossible to ignore the need clawing at me. I wanted to climb back in that bed and ride him until we both passed out from an overdose of orgasms, but that was not in the cards.

Why did it feel like that was never in the cards?

I was staging an official protest.

Turning from him, I stomped toward the door, well aware it probably looked like I was throwing a tantrum. Inside, I definitely was.

Graves' low chuckle told me that he knew it too. The bastard.

But I was basically the reaper version of Batman, and the bat signal was definitely flashing. I couldn't afford to be selfish right now.

"Go put some clothes on or something, I'll find you later," I mutter.

"Salem, I'm already wearing—"

I shut the door on his words and faced off with the door across the hall.

Taking a deep breath, I knocked once and pushed it open.

Abomination

THE ROOM WAS DARK, but the windows were open. Thana lay, staring at the ceiling. In the moonlight, I could see her face clearly. Her expression was blank. Devoid of any emotion.

"I'd wondered which would win out. Your lust for sex or your lust for answers. It seems that the more things change, the more they stay the same." Her words were soft. Spoken in a quiet, almost nostalgic way.

"We need to talk," I said, closing the door behind me. I went to stand over the bed, crossing my arms over my chest. "What was that back there?"

"A warning," Thana answered. I got the impression she was only half paying attention.

"No shit, Sherlock," I snapped.

She snorted. "An ultimatum?" she tried again, her lips curling up even as she did her best to keep her face straight.

"Do you think this is funny?" There was more bite in my tone that time, and the amusement in her features shriveled, turning cold.

"No, but you of all people should understand that humor is easier to handle than sorrow."

I frowned, letting my arms drop to my sides as I sat down on the corner of the bed. "Sorrow? Thana, I don't understand what you're getting at."

She sat up suddenly. "Because it's complicated. Sitting here in your brother's room, I know that as soon as I tell you the truth, you'll betray me."

"What are you talking about?" I asked, my voice going soft to mimic her own.

She smiled bitterly. "The monster, Salem. I'm talking about the monster."

"I'm trying to understand," I said, "but you're speaking in circles—"

"We created the monster, you and I," she said suddenly, as if I hadn't spoken. "At least, in a sense."

The hairs on the back of my neck stood straight. My heart began to pound.

"What is the abomination?" I asked, my voice little more than a hushed whisper.

Thana tilted her head back and smiled. "I'd hoped we had more time. That I could bond with you this go around. But it seems that Death won't even allow us that."

"What is the abomination, Thana?"

"I am."

I blinked. My mouth opening and then closing again. This was all so confusing. Fortunately for me, Thana decided to share.

"Four hundred years ago, you ripped your soul in half. Being a Daughter of Death, neither you nor your soul can die. On the contrary, it heals—and that's exactly what happened. You tore yourself in half and both sides healed. One retained your thoughts and memories and basically everything that made you, well, *you*. The other became me."

"But you said you're my twin . . ."

"Because I might as well be. What are identical twins but an egg and sperm that split into two? You and I shared a soul, Salem. It's not all that different."

Her logic wasn't completely flawed there. I could see how she equated it.

"You lied to me," I said.

"Because you're not ready for the truth. You barely know how to use your powers and now Death is back and knocking on our door. I wanted time with you. To teach you. To get to know you. I didn't want to jump right into this."

"Unfortunately, we don't always get what we want."

She let out a harsh laugh. "Don't I know it."

"Just tell me what's going on," I said, tired of the mind games I'd been playing ever since returning home. "I deserve to know the whole truth."

Out of nowhere, Thana stood up and began pacing.

"You were bored. Lonely. After eons of existing apart from the humans and their world, you wanted a friend. A true companion that could also live forever. You created me, and together we ran Earth . . . for a while. Turns out Death wasn't all that fond about its daughters taking their lives into their own hands. It came to us, demanding that you destroy me. Instead, we destroyed it. At least we thought we did. It should have been obvious we were only granted a temporary reprieve, I mean, if you and I couldn't truly die, how could we believe we'd defeated Death?"

My heart quickened. She could not seriously be telling me—

"The monster is Death."

Okay, that's exactly what she's telling me.

"We tore it apart, but the soul doesn't die. Just like with us, it heals, and Death comes back with a vengeance. Death always comes back."

"What does he want?" I asked.

Thana shrugged one delicate shoulder. "The same thing Death has always wanted; me to be destroyed."

"But *why*?" I asked, feeling like I was missing something.

"Because I am 'the abomination'." She used air quotes, and the sourness in her voice spoke to how difficult this was for her. "I shouldn't exist because Death didn't create me. You did, and therefore, I should be removed. Together we are stronger than even it, but apart . . . well, this is one of many lives you've lived at this point. You get the idea."

"Why do you keep referring to him as an it?"

"Because Death is neither male nor female. Every life it comes back with a different face. A different fake identity. It's a clever bastard. Unlike you, who loses your memories —somehow it has found a way to retain them."

I leaned forward, resting my elbows on my knees. "So how do we defeat it?"

Thana paused in her pacing and looked up. "You want to fight?"

"I didn't say that," I started. "I just want all the information first."

"Death can control ghosts. So now we have the message it sent. First, we have to find out who it is in this life. I was sure that it hadn't reached you yet, which means it's probably hiding among the reapers. Once we find out who it is, we rip it apart."

"You just said that it comes back—"

"After a time. Ripping its soul apart would buy us years before it came back if we do it right," she said in a detached manner. Her lack of emotions was jarring in a way. To hear the words come from my mouth, to see the cold look in my own eyes. She and I were the same . . . and yet not.

A shiver ran through me.

"What do you mean 'do it right'?" I asked softly.

"Not a chance," she replied. "You don't trust me, and you haven't made up your mind about what to do. I'm not telling you the only way to put an immortal down."

"I wouldn't—"

"Kill me?" she asked. Thana smiled, but it wasn't happy. Pain filled her expression then. "You've tried to before. I didn't think it was possible . . . yet here we are again. I don't want to lose you this time, or my own life, so forgive me if I leave out a few things."

I didn't like it, but I couldn't fault her decision either.

"So where do we go from here?" I asked.

"That's entirely up to you," Thana said. "The ghost gave you a week. That's how long you have to figure out how to kill me or to come to grips with the fact that everyone you love is going to die, beside me."

"Unless we shred Death."

Thana nodded.

I'd been in some pretty shitty situations before, but nothing like this.

My options were to try to kill Thana, which I couldn't

imagine would work out even if I wanted to. Or I could let all my friends and family die, if the ghost's warning was to be believed.

Or I could kill Death.

I shook my head, running a hand through my hair. We didn't have a lot of time, and the clock was ticking.

"I need to think," I said, getting up and walking away.

"Don't take too long," Thana said softly behind me.

Leaving Shep's room, I stepped back into the hallway and closed the door behind me. Closing my eyes, I let out one long, deep breath. *Fuck.* Just when I thought things were starting to get under control . . . I guess I should know better than that by now.

Letting my eyes slowly open, I glanced at the door in front of me. The one that would take me back to my room and the sexy reaper laid out on my bed. There was a weird sort of irony about finding myself in a hallway filled with doors right now. If I believed in things like life metaphors, I'd say this was a pretty obvious one.

I had a choice to make, and sadly, it wasn't going to be as easy as choosing between having fun with Graves, or scavenging for emergency cupcakes in the kitchen.

No . . . the consequences of the choices before me were much more serious. And no matter which option I chose . . . someone was going to die. It should be easy . . . right? Pick the one that saves the most people. That's what a good person would do.

But was I a good person?

After what happened with James, I wasn't really sure anymore.

The In-between

ESME WAS FIDDLING with some kind of steampunk goggles when I stumbled into the kitchen the next morning. Graves was still in the shower, and Thana was nowhere to be seen. For the moment, I had my aunt to myself.

"Cosplaying?" I guessed, moving toward the coffeepot.

Esme snorted. "Even better. I finally have a reason to work on my ghost goggles."

"Your what?" I asked, looking up from the steaming liquid in my mug, not certain I had heard her correctly.

"Ghost goggles. You need to be able to see the enemy if you're going to fight it."

As always, she never ceased to surprise me.

"Okay, but how are you planning to fight one when you still can't touch them?" I asked.

"Easy," she said, sparing me a quick look. "You trap them."

Coffee bubbled out of my mouth as I started coughing. The image of my aunt as a Ghostbuster had taken root in my mind, and I couldn't stop laughing.

Setting her ghost-fighting equipment down, Esme walked over and slapped me hard on the back. "Easy there."

"I'm good," I said, my voice still a little froggy. "Just went down the wrong pipe."

"You never were good at multitasking," she said breezily, moving away from me.

"All I was doing was sipping my coffee," I protested.

"While you were also trying to figure out how to trap a ghost. It was too much for you. You really should be more careful."

I gaped at my aunt, not sure if she was teasing me or insulting me. Knowing her, it was probably a bit of both.

"Morning," Graves said, joining us. He eyed Esme and her project curiously before heading over to me and grabbing a cup of his own.

"Esme is preparing for a ghost hunt," I informed him.

"As one does," Graves muttered, totally unfazed.

I had to hand it to him, he was already a total pro when it came to Esme and her hobbies.

"What are you two—three," she corrected as Thana made her appearance, "up to today?"

"We," Graves said, gesturing to the two of us, "have that emergency Council meeting this morning. The new reps are being presented, and they're going to revote on what to do about the werewolf."

I frowned. As important as that was, it paled in comparison after what happened last night. "I think I need to spend some time with Thana. She promised to teach me more about my powers. With everything going on, I'm pretty sure I'm going to need to level up some more."

"And by level up, you mean die?" Graves concluded.

I shrugged. "Do you know of another way?"

"No, but that doesn't mean there isn't one."

I glanced over at Thana. My doppelgänger sighed. "Not in this case, unfortunately."

"There you have it."

Graves pressed his lips together, clearly not very happy about her response.

"The Council meeting wasn't a choice, Salem—"

"We only have one week," I replied, steel in my voice. "I don't like it. But I need to level up fast and learn as much as I can about this monster if we're going to—"

"She's the one it wants." Esme nodded toward Thana.

My sister blinked once, masking her surprise behind the purse of her lips. "How'd you gather that?" Thana asked.

"I have eyes."

I lifted both brows. "Esme, that's—"

"Well done, Reaper." Thana nodded. "At least one of you has intelligence." She side-eyed Graves, whose jaw looked like it was soldered together at this point.

His eyes were all on me.

"She's the abomination it spoke of?" he asked.

"Well, it's . . . complicated."

"So uncomplicate it."

I crossed my arms over my chest. "Look, there's a lot going on right now, and we don't have a lot of time—"

"You're making excuses," Graves interrupted, his voice clipped.

"Excuse me?" I snapped.

"He's right, you know," Esme said, nodding along beside us.

"Did you just"—I let out a harsh breath—"of course

you did." I pinched the bridge of my nose between my fingers. "Look, the monster may want Thana, but it's not her fault."

"Oh, I sincerely doubt that," Graves said.

"Must I remind you of your mortality—" Thana started.

"Stop it," I snapped. "Both of you. Graves, you're going to the meeting. I'm staying here with Thana to learn more about my powers. Esme—"

"I'm laying a trap for the next time our friends decide to visit," my aunt said.

"Alright, that's that."

"I don't know about this, Salem," Graves started.

"Trust me," I said. "I need to do this."

We weren't alone, but when our eyes met, it felt like we were. His seemed to glow for a moment before he nodded once.

"This isn't over."

The corner of my mouth tugged up. "I'd expect nothing less."

"Focus. You are nothingness. Empty. Obsolete," Thana instructed.

I let out an exasperated breath. "I'm trying, but it isn't as easy as you think it is."

"We came from the void. It was where we were created. It is where we will always return," she said.

I opened my eyes to see a ghostly version of myself standing before me, with arms crossed over her chest.

"I don't even know what that means." I sighed, the tension of trying to turn myself into my ghost form draining away.

"Death created its daughters by putting a piece of itself inside a female from each species that controlled the realm the daughter would oversee. A seed of power that blossomed into a goddess." Thana walked around me as she spoke. "Upon birth, every mother died, taking Death's babe with her. You were reborn in the afterworld and raised by Death. Then you were sent to the Earth once more, where for eons you were the only one of your kind. Alone."

Her ghostly fingers brushed over my shoulder, and I felt *something* as she did so.

My shoulder tingled.

"Until you got the idea to do the same," Thana continued. "Except you are not Death. Not completely. You split your soul in the in-between and waited for it to heal. When it was whole once more, I was here. Just like this." She motioned to herself, dressed in ripped skinny jeans and a graphic tee. "Not a ghost, but a god. We came from the nothingness, Salem. We can return to it."

I closed my eyes once more and focused on just letting go.

I envisioned my body fading away. My soul becoming nothing.

As a hint of despair started to fill me, I felt it. An awareness that spread through me, filling me. Recreating me. A heaviness settled inside me before lifting and giving way to weightlessness.

I opened my eyes and the world was leached of color.

Thana was grinning. "Welcome to the in-between, Salem."

"Weird," I breathed, looking down at my body that now had the same spectral quality as hers. "So we can just come and go here whenever we want?"

She nodded. "Think of it as a shortcut."

"A shortcut to what?" I asked.

"Everything."

She'd lost me again.

"I thought this was like . . ." I trailed off, not having the words. "You know . . . a place that exists separate from the real world."

"It does. Technically, it's the spirit world; a place that all spirits return to once they leave your realm, but before they move on to their final destinations, as it were. Since you are in charge of all the souls on Earth, you can move freely between all of them. You can go anywhere that a soul can. On Earth, however, you are limited by its natural laws, physics, if you will."

I blinked at her. "Why don't you try that again using smaller words," I said.

Thana smirked. "If you wanted to go to Antarctica, how would you get there?"

"Why would I want to go to Antarctica?"

"Salem," she said with exasperation.

"Okay fine, um . . . I guess I'd fly? Or get there by boat? And then use a dogsled or something."

"Or, you could come to this realm and be there in less time than it takes to draw a full breath."

It clicked then, what she'd meant by shortcut.

"All you have to do is think about where you want to go and"—she snapped her fingers—"you're there."

I remembered the forest. Seeing the werewolf and knowing I didn't have time to make it to him before he attacked, but somehow I'd just managed to appear before him in the nick of time.

"That is so fucking cool."

She was smiling again. "So, Salem. Where do you want to go?"

My mind was blank for a second before a mischievous grin stretched across my face. "Let's go spy on Graves."

Thana rolled her eyes but nodded. "Alright, picture him. Hold his image firmly in your mind. Focus on it. Once you do it a few times, it won't require much more than a thought, but it's a good way to learn."

I thought about Graves lying on my bed and felt an answering flutter low in my stomach. Alright, maybe I needed something less distracting. Instead, I focused on his spearmint and aftershave smell. The feel of his hand brushing low against my back.

"Good job," Thana said, interrupting my happy thoughts and sending my eyes fluttering open.

We weren't in a grayed-out version of my house anymore, but standing at the grayed-out back of the Council meeting. In this form, I was like a fly on the wall. No one could see or hear me.

Graves was standing on my right, his face set in a scowl and his arms crossed over his chest. He was obviously unhappy with whatever the fae woman was saying.

"How come I can't hear anything?" I asked her, as I watched Nocturna's mouth moving on the stage.

"You can, you're just focused on me and this realm right now, so everything else is muted. Think of it like needing to turn up the volume."

"With what remote, Thana?" I asked sarcastically.

"You're the remote, Salem," she replied, matching my tone perfectly.

Creepy.

"I don't know what that means, but whatever. Let's give it a go." I stared hard at Nocturna, focusing on her lips and my desire to hear what she was saying.

"No, Salem—" Thana started.

The world bounced back into stunning color. I squinted my eyes, not prepared for the sudden shift back into high definition.

"Salem, what the hell are you doing here?" Graves asked beside me.

Shit. Guess I didn't nail that lesson.

"Uh, hey. What'd I miss?"

Overturned

"WE SHALL CALL IT TO A VOTE," a voice I recognized rang out. I peered over the heads of supes to see Nocturna standing at the head of the table. Her lavender hair was worn long, sections from the top pulled into tiny braids and then woven around her head to form a crown. Black flowers were interlaced, matching the ensemble she wore.

"All in favor of execution?"

At once, the thrill of being with Thana faded as the harsh reality of what was going on started to set in.

Tamsin kept her hand lowered, as did the new warlock and female werewolf representatives.

The vampire who had spoken out yesterday, Rembrandt, raised his hand.

The female dwarf raised her hand.

Nocturna raised her hand.

And Dom raised his.

"Son of a bitch," I cursed, my hands balling into fists. Graves grabbed my forearm, pulling me back against his chest.

Nocturna was talking, but I didn't hear it.

"Wait until we're back at the Grimm house. They won't respect him if you go after him here, and it won't win us any favors." Graves' words washed over me, grounding me in the moment.

"Or," another voice said. I glanced sideways. Thana stood in her ghostly form, arms over her chest. "You could show them who you are. What you are. Their ruling is nothing compared to the will of a goddess."

I frowned, narrowing my eyes. "That's not how we do things here."

"And you're such a rule follower?" Thana replied in the same scathing tone. When I didn't respond, her lips quirked up. "Didn't think so."

"There's a difference in not wanting to follow rules and wanting to make them," I shot back. Several heads turned my way, and Graves' fingers tightened.

"Thana or Gretel?" he asked softly, his lips brushing against my ear. The words were barely more than a whisper as he worked to keep his voice quiet enough no one would hear us.

"Who do you think?" I asked under my breath.

"My least favorite demigoddess, then," he replied.

Thana narrowed her eyes. *Yup. She totally heard that.*

"He's a bad influence on you," she said.

I scoffed. "*He* is? Seriously?"

She nodded, completely serious. "He lives by their rules, Salem. The Grimm Brotherhood is his legacy. He will conform you to them, so that you'll be complacent. He'll make you weak."

"He's never tried to change me," I hissed back at her.

She lifted both brows. Her eyes flicked down to the hand holding my arm. A devious smile curled around her lips, but it was bitter. "Hasn't he?"

Thana disappeared, and I let out a string of curses that would have drawn more attention were the room not clearing.

"Motherfucking vague-booking sister—"

"I take it she left?" Graves asked, releasing my arm.

I blew out a breath. "Yup. Maybe I should go after her . . ."

"Graves. Kaine."

I glanced across the room at Dom. His eyes were hard. My original anger toward him for reversing the vote came back.

"Nice of you to show up," he continued in his dry, arrogant tone.

"Not even one day in your new role and you're already sentencing innocent people to death, Dom. Way to ring in a new era of peace and acceptance."

His eyes narrowed and deep lines bracketed his mouth. "This is not the time or the place for your shitty attitude. Not that I need to explain anything to you, but that wolf is far from innocent. Sure, he may have been coerced into the most recent murders, but that first one was all him. The law is clear, and so is the punishment."

I scowled, sliding my arms across my chest, about to lay into him when Graves' fingers pressed into my hip.

"You don't really think they're just going to hand him over," Graves said in a carefully neutral voice.

Dom shrugged. "Not my problem. The Council gave them until sundown tomorrow to bring the kid in—which is more than we had to give them," he added, glaring at me. "They don't show, the reapers will go in and get him."

"Dom, you can't let that happen. It's practically a declaration of war," I insisted as the scenario played out in gory detail in my mind. The wolves would take it as a sign of aggression if the reapers invaded their land to search for Gerard. Everyone knew wolves were territorial. It didn't take a genius to see how such an act would end.

"If it is, we aren't the ones making the declaration. Reapers enforce the law. As long as everyone follows the rules, there's no need to enforce them, is there?"

I was shaking my head, his logic so black and white, and so utterly wrong. "You can't be that stupid," I said.

He glared at me. "Watch that pretty mouth of yours, Kaine."

"Or what? You're going to execute me too? Good luck with that, Fuckface. Don't make me out to be the enemy because I call you on your bullshit. This is fucked up, and you know it."

Dom sighed. "I didn't ask for this, but if I recall correctly, your hand was in the air backing me. So fucking back me, Salem."

I froze, my mouth opening and closing like a fish at his words, permeating the anger clouding my mind. He was right. I had chosen him. I just hadn't expected him to disappoint me so quickly.

It was my turn to sigh. "I thought you would be a little more open-minded. Was I wrong?"

Dom and I shared a look. I wouldn't say it was friendly, but there was a sort of grudging respect there.

"You may not agree with me, but at least trust that I'm

doing what I believe is right, not just for the reapers, but for Farrow's Square. Believe it or not, Kaine, I'm trying to *avoid* a war."

My shoulders sagged, the last of my anger fleeing. "Fine. But when this goes to shit, you bet your ass I'm saying I told you so."

"You? Really? How out of character." He gave me a smug grin.

I glared at him.

"Why'd you call us over here?" Graves asked, moving the conversation into smoother territory.

"I need people to watch the werewolf property to make sure they don't try to smuggle him out. Given your father voted for him to live, they will hold less of a grudge against you." Dom nodded toward Graves, his expression guarded. It occurred to me he may actually be telling the truth here. I just didn't understand his endgame.

"You want me to lead the patrol," Graves surmised.

"Correct." Dom nodded. "Kaine needs to stay behind, though."

"What?"

"You remember our talk yesterday?" Dom lowered his voice.

"So? If there's trouble, I should be there—"

"I agree," Graves said. "Salem should stay behind."

Real outrage filled me as I turned on Graves.

"You've gotta be fucking kidding me—"

"Someone needs to watch Esme."

"What? Esme"—I paused, realizing he was really talking about Thana. There were things he didn't know, though. Like the fact she could literally be anywhere in the world at any time with only a thought. Meanwhile Death was out there . . .

"Esme is a grown adult who does what she wants," I said eventually.

"You weren't telling me that earlier," Graves replied, an edge entering his tone.

"I'm not my aunt's keeper," I fired back.

"Well, that's unfortunate because either way you're staying behind. You care too much about this, Kaine, and I can't have you interfering right now. For better or worse, you need to sit this one out." Dom put a hand on my shoulder, but I shrugged it off.

Turning on my heel, I started for the door.

"Where are you going?" Graves called out.

"To do what you said," I replied. "Keep an eye on my *aunt*."

I thrust the door open and stepped into the empty hallway. It slammed shut behind me. Closing my eyes, I focused on being nothing. Feeling nothing.

It came easy this time.

Easier than it should have.

Graves' footsteps faded as the world of the dead welcomed me. I opened my eyes right as the door burst open.

Graves looked up and down the hall. Surprise filling his features.

He can't see me like this, I realized. Given how fast things happened when I first showed up with Thana, I wasn't quite sure.

I didn't want to hurt him. Well, not much anyways. I cared about Graves. More than I was ready to admit, especially when him and Dom were being so stupid about this whole thing. If Dom was so insistent I needed to stay away, and Graves was going to side with him, I wasn't letting either of them off easy. Just because I voted for the fucker didn't mean he got to decide how I was running my life.

Graves was right that I needed to keep an eye on Thana. Much as I hated to give him any credit.

What he didn't realize was that in this form, I could kill two birds with one stone.

And that's exactly what I planned to do.

"WHEN YOU TOLD me we were going spying on Graves, I thought it was going to be a little more exciting," Thana said, leaning against a tree and inspecting her nails.

We'd been out here for a few hours now, and so far it was about as exciting as watching a slug race.

"How was I supposed to know all they were going to do was walk in circles for hours on end?"

"Didn't you patrol with him? Isn't this what you're used to?"

Thoughts of a succubus house party came to mind, and I smiled. "Patrol was usually a bit livelier in my experience."

Thana hummed. "What would your lover say if he knew you were spying on him?"

Graves would be pissed. Not at the invasion of privacy, since this was patrol and not alone time—although surprising Graves in the shower could be fun—but that I'd gone against his wishes. "About as happy as you'd expect," I muttered.

"Why are you allowing a man to control you?" she asked, pushing off the tree and giving me her full attention.

I eyed Graves and Randy, who were talking in low voices a few yards away.

"I don't let him control me, but I respect him and his advice. There's a difference."

"Is there?" she sneered. "From where I'm standing, you're hiding in the shadows, afraid of upsetting a couple of reapers. Do you have any idea how powerful you are? You shouldn't be afraid of anyone, Salem. They should fear you."

"Not even Death?" I countered, wiping that condescending smile right off her face.

"That's different, and you know it."

"Do I?"

She scowled at me, throwing her hands in the air. "Sometimes I wonder why I ever missed you. You're a giant pain in the ass."

I laughed at that, wholly unoffended. My friends and family have been telling me that for years. "Right back 'atcha, Sis."

"I mean it, Salem. You're wasting your talents skulking about like this. You are a goddess. If you want something, take it. If you disagree with something, put an end to it. Why the games?"

I could tell by the frustration in her voice that she really didn't understand. Just like with Dom, it was black and white for her.

"Because sometimes, Thana, to get what you want, you have to work within someone else's boundaries."

"Why?"

"Because," I snapped, "I'm not the only person who lives here. I can't just go around ordering everybody to obey me. That's not how peace works. That's not how relationships work."

"And how is hiding in the spirit world getting you any closer to obtaining your goals?"

At the moment? It wasn't, but I wasn't about to tell her that.

"Right now, we're keeping an eye on the reapers, while they keep an eye on the wolves. If anything gets out of hand, we'll be able to step in and save the day. It's a failsafe."

"It's boring."

"You can leave whenever you want."

We'd gotten so distracted by our bickering that we didn't notice the porch light turning on up ahead. Graves and Randy had gone completely still in front of us as the back door to one of the houses slid open.

"You planning to wait out here all night?" a masculine voice called. A hulking form, backlit by the light inside, filled the doorframe.

Graves' jaw tightened. "Just doing our job," he called back.

"I'll take that as a yes." The figure stepped outside. I recognized the old pack representative. His grey hair reflected in the moonlight. Shadows played off the scar on his face, making him appear menacing, if not for the slightly amused expression. "Why don't you come inside?"

"I don't think that's a good idea—" Graves started.

"You got any food?" Randy asked.

The werewolf nodded. "We ordered pizza."

Like any good pothead, Randy's feet were moving before his brain ever had a chance.

Graves reached out to stop him. "We're supposed to be patrolling."

"Really, man? I know you and Salem spent most of your patrol time at the succubus house. I'm not one to judge . . . but don't give me shit." Randy shrugged Graves off.

Graves' jaw tightened, and he followed after his stoner friend.

"Your lover in this life is a real stick in the mud," Thana said.

"He takes his job seriously," I answered defensively.

My doppelgänger rolled her eyes, clearly not impressed by that answer. "He's not your usual type," she continued, starting toward the cabin after them.

I kept pace alongside her. "My usual type?"

"Mhmm," she hummed. "You like them smart, a bit arrogant, *strong*." That last bit came out in a sexual purr that would have given Tamsin a run for her money.

"You clearly don't know Graves if you don't see how that fits."

"Perhaps," she said, walking through the back door.

I followed suit. Inside, both reapers sat at a large dinner table, stacked high with boxes. The werewolf rep sat across from them.

Thana took my silence as an excuse to continue with her storytelling. "In your last life, you had a werewolf lover. An alpha. He was a possessive one. You liked that. Mostly because you liked pushing his buttons." She strolled forward, walking around the table, her eyes focused on

Graves, who had no idea we were here. "Before that, it was warlocks. Two of them. Brothers. You enjoyed pitting them against each other to win your affection. You did that in a few of your lives, took multiple lovers. Only ones that couldn't play nicely, though. It was a game for you. Love always has been."

"That doesn't sound much like me," I said, unsure what else to say to that.

"Doesn't it, though? You like this one because you like arguing with him. Once that fades, you'll get bored. You always do. It's the curse of being an immortal." She trailed her nails along the edge of the table. "Even if you do believe me, and we do manage to kill Death, and he hasn't bored you in a few years, you won't age. He will. And for a time, that might work. You've had your stints with old men over the eons. But they are mortal. If not by boredom then by death, you will eventually leave him and find another."

"Why are you so set on driving a wedge between him and I?" I asked her pointedly.

Thana paused. Her neutral expression breaking into a smile. "You might be immortal, but you've lived as a mortal in this life. Losing him will be hard for a time, because of how attached you are. I'd rather save you that heartache."

"Mhmm," I hummed, mocking her. "How kind."

Thana's eyes narrowed. "It may not seem like a kindness to you in the moment, but trust me, Sister, better to leave him to his mortal existence now than to waste your immortal one mourning for a man you cannot have."

The men at the table were talking, and I knew I should be paying attention, but something about the catch in Thana's voice had me riveted. This was a woman who'd clearly had her heart broken—stomped on, from the sound of it—and in her own, cold way, she was trying to protect me.

Then something she said registered. "Why can't I have him? If we control souls, what keeps me from helping Graves remain in this world . . ." Graves and I had the blood rite that tied us together. Not that Thana knew that. But to keep someone in this world, well, there was another I very much wanted to do that for. "For that matter," I said with excitement as an idea took shape, "what's keeping me from just sucking Shep back into this world the way Death does with his ghosts? If Death doesn't need a new body to give souls physical form, why do we?"

Thana was frowning, her brows dipping low over her eyes as she considered my question. "We are not Death, Salem."

"No, but you said together we are more powerful than Death. Powerful enough to defeat him. Maybe we could pull this off if we tried."

Her frown deepened. She was not a fan of my plan, that much was obvious. But what I didn't understand was why.

"You know the pack will never willingly hand over one of its members," the gray-haired werewolf said, interrupting our ghostly debate.

"And you know the Council will never accept that," Graves said, his voice a perfect, matter-of-fact match to the wolf's.

The older wolf nodded, like he expected as much.

Graves sighed. "Eli, you know I don't agree with the decision. You also know I'm not a dumbass." His eyes shifted to Randy, who was all but inhaling a box of pizza and paying zero attention.

Eli and Graves shared an amused smile, but Graves' fell as quickly as it appeared.

"If I look out the window right now, am I going to see Gerard sneaking off?" Graves asked.

Eli shrugged. "Could you blame him if he was?"

"This is all so tedious," Thana said beside me, starting to pace.

Graves sighed. "Off the record? No. If it were me, I'd try to run. On the record? I can't let that happen, Eli. You also know we aren't the only two reapers out here. He's not going to get far, and it will only make things worse for the pack."

Moving to the window, I glanced outside, but I didn't notice any shadowy figures sneaking around.

Graves sat back, his expression resigned. "Don't make this harder than it already is."

Eli took a sip of something I was assuming was whisky, given the color and the massive ice cube sitting at the bottom of the glass. "We all have our parts to play, Reaper. The rest is up to fate."

Eli reached around behind him and pulled out a firearm.

Aw fuck.

Martyr

"Randy?" Graves said, his voice tight.

Randy was a bit preoccupied. I hadn't noticed before now because I wasn't paying much attention myself.

His hands shook. The glass of water he'd been holding toppled sideways. Water hit the hardwood floors as tremors racked his body. Randy collapsed sideways, shaking, but immobile.

"You drugged him." Graves' tone was neutral. Apathetic. He didn't act afraid or even concerned for his own life in the slightest. I mean, why would he? Not when Eli couldn't kill him. At least not long-term.

"He's going to take a little nap while you and I have a chat."

"Well, well, now this is getting interesting," Thana said.

"This isn't going to end well. You have to know that," Graves said, trying to reason with him.

"You're going to make a call," Eli replied, ignoring his words entirely. "To your buddies out there. Let them know I've got you right here at gunpoint."

Graves frowned. "Gerard might get away, but that won't stop them from coming down on you."

"I know."

Now it was my turn to frown.

"I don't think he deserves execution, but that kid is a killer, Eli. You know that as well as I do. He's not innocent in this, and he's sure as hell not worth you going down for."

Eli chuckled. It didn't sound evil or malicious or maniacal. It sounded . . . like a regular guy having a regular conversation. "I know what he did, Graves. I know everything. Including the role your own brother played in this entire fiasco—a fact that has been magically left out, courtesy of your dad. He and I had a deal, you see. My wolf gets to live, and the public doesn't have to know his own son was a fucking psycho."

Stone would have shown more expression than Graves did at that little revelation.

"And my brother was executed for his crimes."

"You see, that's just it, though. The reapers have decided what happens to the rest of us for as long as anyone can remember. It wasn't your father's or anyone else's choice to decide what happened to James. That should have been done by the Council. But once again, the reapers took matters into their own hands. Just like you did with Gerard's older brother."

I was only a few seconds from popping into existence right there and showing this asshole the other end of my boot, but his words stopped me cold.

Even behind his mask of indifference, a look crossed Graves' face. It was fleeting, but there.

And in that split second, I knew. Eli wasn't lying.

"I don't blame you, Graves. You're a product of the world you've grown up in. I, and all other members of the Council, allowed your father to do these things off the books in return for small courtesies that were nothing compared to the crimes committed against our people. *I* am the reason Gerard's brother died and never got justice. *I* am the reason he was filled with so much anger, and I will not allow him to be executed for it."

"This is going to start a war," Graves said eventually.

"It already has," Eli replied. "Now make the call. No sudden moves—and if you so much as think to reach for your gun—I'll shoot you."

Graves pulled his cell out of his pocket and hit a button without taking his eyes off of the wolf holding the gun.

"Sam? We have a situation." Graves fell silent for a beat before adding, "Randy's been poisoned, and there's an angry wolf with a gun pointed right at me." He paused again. "Eli's, yeah." Then he hung up. "They're on their way, just like you wanted."

Eli gave Graves a slow, easy smile. "Good, good. Had things gone differently, you and I might have been friends or, at the very least, allies. As things stand, can't say I hate you. Can't say I like you much either," he added, his smile lifting higher on one side.

"You just going to stand here and watch this guy kill your boyfriend? No judgment if you are. Good riddance, but you know . . . apathy seems more like my thing than yours," Thana said.

I shot her a quick glare. "Of course I'm not just going to stand here and wait for him to die, but if I just pop into existence, I might startle the guy enough he accidentally pulls the trigger."

"So use that to your advantage. Maybe he'll shoot you. It could be like a win-win. Your boyfriend lives, and you get to power up."

The metallic click as he cocked the gun told me I was out of time. Without a second thought, I launched myself at the wolf, coming back onto their plane in time to tackle him.

The gun went off with a loud crack, and I hissed in pain as a bullet grazed my arm.

"What the fuck?" Eli cried out, grunting as we slammed into the floor.

"Salem?" Graves asked, more confused than anything.

"Uh, surprise," I said, pushing myself up off a dazed Eli.

He blinked up at me before scowling. "One reaper or two, doesn't matter to me. I won't let you take me alive."

He lifted the gun, aiming it straight at my face.

I didn't think; I just kicked out, breaking his wrist with the force of the blow and sending the gun flying from his hand. "How about no one has to die?"

Eli let out a garbled scream, cradling his broken wrist against his chest. "You fucking reaper bitch."

"Yeah yeah, heard that one before. Be more original."

"Salem, what are you doing here?" Graves asked, blood dripping down from the graze on his arm.

"Saving your ass. You're welcome, by the way."

Graves stared at me. "You've been keeping secrets."

I raised a brow. "For like . . . five hours."

"You and I are having a talk when we get out of here."

Thana popped into being beside me. "You two talk too

much. What are you doing standing around? That guy just tried to kill you. Twice. Why is he still alive?"

Graves' eyes went wide as he looked from me to my twin. "You brought her with you? What was this, a fucking field trip?"

Eli was groaning below us as he tried to roll onto his stomach and start crawling for his weapon. I stepped on his injured arm. "Not so fast, buddy."

"Salem," Graves said again. His voice hard. "Why the fuck is Thana here?"

"We're hanging out," I said, looking between him and the injured werewolf I was pinning to the ground with my boot. Even James had a higher pain tolerance than this dude. He really should have thought twice before trying to bring down the reapers on him. "I figured I could kill two birds with one stone."

"You're not supposed to be here," Graves said.

"Yeah, well, look how that would have turned out for you if I wasn't." I pressed my lips together, giving him a pointed look.

A gun shot rang out.

I froze.

She did not just—

"You should spend more time with your aunt. Lady of action, that one is," Thana said, tossing the gun.

Graves caught it in one hand. "You just killed a man," he said.

Across the room, a ghost popped up.

He looked confused for a moment, taking in the scene, and then his own dead body.

Thana shrugged. "He wanted to die anyway."

"Just because he wanted to die doesn't mean we just—"

"What? Kill him?" my twin responded, then let out a harsh chuckle. "Newsflash, reaper boy. He knew about Salem and me. Since you two are so insistent on pretending she's only a reaper, it was the only way. Besides. He tried to kill you. While I don't think you're good for my sister, you do seem to have her attention for the moment, and being mortal and all . . . well, ghosts don't make for good fuck buddies." Thana turned and walked past us both, the heels of her boots clicking against the wooden floor. She leaned forward and lifted one of the blinds to glance through the window.

"We need to go," I said.

Graves looked from her to me, a sliver of shock slipping through his mask.

"Salem, she just—"

"I know what she did," I snapped. "And while I don't agree with it, she's right. He's dead, and I can't lie for shit, so we need to get out of here. Not make this any worse than it already is."

"You could put him back," Graves said quietly. Blue fire shone in his eyes as he stared at me.

"I could," I said slowly, then looked away. "But where would that get us? He'll run his mouth and word will get out about what I am. What if it makes everything worse?"

Graves' jaw clenched. "Then we deal with it."

"I—" I paused, searching for words I was struggling to find, but knew they wouldn't come. I glanced at Thana, and she merely shrugged.

"Put him back or not, the choice is yours."

I knew right then that this was a test. By killing him, she

forced my hand. Either I put his soul back and he tells the whole supernatural world my secret, or I leave him dead and prove just how far I'll go.

Icy anger filled me.

This was all a game to her.

And now I was left with the choice of deciding whether Eli should stay dead or not.

Except I was out of time.

"I'm not an idiot. I may not remember who I used to be, and maybe she was a callous bitch—but I'm not playing these games with you. You may be my sister, but who I am now is not okay with this." I motioned to the dead body. "If this is your way of trying to show me who you are so I don't choose Death, you're doing a piss-poor job."

"Salem, I—" She choked up, tears forming at the corners of her eyes.

"Save it," I growled.

The tears dried instantly. "You need to make some choices, Sister. You may not see it this way, but I was trying to help."

"I don't need this kind of help."

Thana lifted one delicate shoulder and shrugged. "We'll see."

She morphed into her spirit form and then disappeared entirely.

I stormed over to Eli's ghost, not wasting the precious few seconds I had left. "If I give you a second chance, what are you going to do with it?"

Eli stared at me, his lips lifted in an apologetic smile, the corners of eyes creasing slightly. "Whatever I have to in order to keep my people safe."

Regret sat heavy in my stomach. "I'm sorry, Graves." I turned to face him, pleading with my eyes for him to forgive me. "I can't bring him back. His intentions might be honorable, but it will be disastrous, and not just for the reapers. We stand a better chance of keeping the peace without him."

Graves' face was stormy, his eyes twin bolts of lightning. "What's done is done now, Salem. Just . . . get out of here. I'll deal with this mess and come find you afterward."

The sound of footsteps racing up the stairs filled the silence between us, and I pulled myself back, willing myself into the spirit realm just as the door to Eli's house flew open and reapers stormed in.

I let myself stay there unseen long enough for Graves to show his brothers the gun. I watched as his lips formed the words 'self-defense' and then I pulled myself away.

It was my mess he was cleaning up, and it wasn't sitting well with me. For the first time since learning I was a Daughter of Death, I felt the true burden of my power. Who was I to decide whether someone deserved to live or die? I was hardly the poster child for good decision-making. If anything, I was the exact opposite.

Eli wasn't James. His death wasn't some kind of cosmic justice. I'd been given a choice, and there was no obvious right answer.

But not choosing wasn't an option, and now I had to deal with the fallout.

One-Woman Show

"Say something."

I stared at Tamsin as she opened and closed her mouth. The third time she shook her head and blew out a breath.

"You lead the craziest life out of anyone I know, and I live with sex vampires."

I cracked a grin, absentmindedly reaching out and patting the bed, checking for more cupcakes. Only empty wrappers and colored lingerie came up. I groaned. Where was the food when I needed it?

"You think it'll ever slow down?" I asked her, flopping back on her king-sized bed. The fluorescent light glared down on me, and I wrinkled my nose. I'd never noticed things like that before, but it covered everything in a hazy film.

"I mean, doesn't life usually?" Tam asked. I couldn't see her, but I could imagine her sitting cross-legged on the floor, staring at me with amusement.

"For normal people." I frowned. "They grow up and

settle down, have a couple of kids, and grow old together . . ." I said, my voice trailing off.

That would never be me. I hadn't thought much about it since finding out I was immortal, not just long-lived like most of the supes. Truly immortal. Which means even if I wanted to die one day, I couldn't. It was a strange thing, and oddly morbid, given I was talking about living and dying for once.

"That's one road," Tam said. I heard her shuffling around, and then her head popped up. She climbed onto the bed next to me. "But it's not the only one. This isn't the eighteen-hundreds anymore. You don't *have* to get married. You don't *have* to have kids, you don't *have* to do anything. You can choose who you want to be."

"All within Farrow's Square."

She nodded, a sad smile dotting her lips as she repeated, "All within Farrow's Square."

"Maybe Farrow's Square is the problem," I said. "My life has always been kind of complicated, but things weren't crazy until I came home."

"Do you regret it?" she asked without judgment.

"No." I twisted my lips. "If anything, I wish I came back sooner. Or never left. Things might have happened differently then . . . but I can't change the past."

"Nope," Tamsin agreed. "You can't, but you can decide on your future. Fix things with Graves. Deal with your semi-psychotic twin. Bring back your much more reasonable twin. Those are things you can do."

"Assuming Death doesn't just kill everyone," I griped.

Tamsin's lips pressed together. She put on a good face, but I could tell that part was bothering her. "Well, there is that. Assuming you even wanted to kill Thana, though, could you? Is there a way to truly kill your kind?"

I exhaled heavily. "There's gotta be one, but I don't know it, and while I don't really care for Thana . . ."

"You don't want to kill her," Tamsin finished for me.

I nodded. "Does that make me a bad person? I mean—I wanted to kill James. I left Eli dead, but something in me butts against killing her. It's like killing Shep. She was my twin once—or close to it—and clearly a lot has happened that's made her this way. And who's to say that Death doesn't just want her out of the way so he can take me out too?"

Tamsin sat up, her lithe brown arms draped across her legs.

"It's not an easy situation you're in. I don't envy you," Tamsin started.

"But?" I prompted, sensing it coming.

She grinned. "But I think the only way you're going to find out these answers is from Death or Thana herself. Maybe both, really. If there's anything I know, it's that there are more sides to the story. I can compel two people who saw the same thing to tell me the truth, and their narratives are almost always different because people's perspectives are different."

I thought about that, and wondered—was there a way to talk to them both? I mean, Thana was convinced that one of the reapers was actually Death. The only one who would know for sure though was . . . the ghosts.

As if I summoned him by thought alone, Shep appeared in front of me.

"Graves is looking for you."

Ugh. Talk about difficult situations I'd rather avoid. I'd purposely talked about everything but him.

"Not very hard," I muttered, sitting up and swinging my legs over the side of the bed, sending crumpled plastic wrappers and a few bras tumbling to the floor.

"What was that?" Tamsin asked.

"Shep," I said with a sigh.

"Hey girl hey," Shepard said to Tamsin, giving her a wave that resembled jazz hands.

"She can't see you, dumbass."

"Doesn't mean I can't be polite," he retorted. "Do your job; act as my interpreter."

I rolled my eyes. "Shep is giving you the fingers."

"Hey!" Shep protested.

"The fingers?" Tamsin asked, her nose scrunching in confusion.

I mimed his stupid wiggling finger wave.

Tamsin's expression cleared, and she laughed. "God, I've missed you two buttheads going at each other. You guys were like . . . my favorite reality TV show."

"I'm so glad we entertain you," I said dryly, my eyes drifting back to Shep. "Are you really just here to let me know Graves is on the prowl, or is there something else you wanted?"

"Can't a brother just want to check in on his sister when she's not fucking his best friend?" Shep asked.

I raised a brow. "Is that brother you?"

Shep grinned at me. "I really was here to let you know about Graves. Silly me, I thought you might care that your boyfriend was looking for you. Guess there's trouble in paradise already." He paused and snapped his fingers. "But now that you mention it, maybe we could pencil in a time to take care of that body issue of mine." He gave me a pointed look.

I was groaning and shaking my head at his assessment of my relationship with Graves when the rest of what he said sunk in. "Hey! I want to try something." I jumped to my feet and tried to grab my brother by the arm.

Tingles raced through my body, but my hand passed through without making physical contact.

I frowned.

"Salem, as much as I love these one-woman shows you put on when you're chatting up your ghost friends, what the hell are you doing now?" Tamsin asked.

"Something Thana mentioned gave me an idea," I said, staring hard at my twin and trying to will him back into existence. Nothing. I sighed. "I was hoping I might be able to use my power to help Shep manifest physically without needing a new body, but I don't actually have a fucking clue how that works. I was hoping I could just sort of . . . pull him back into the land of the living. Guess I'm going to need to think on that more . . ." I added, mostly speaking to myself. *Or ask Thana to help me.* My lips dipped into a frown. I didn't want to ask her for any favors right now. After the shit she pulled with Eli, she was even lower on the list of people I wanted to talk to than Graves was.

Both Tamsin and Shepard started laughing at me.

"What?" I snapped, jerking out of my thoughts.

"Nothing, sweetie," Tamsin said, pretending to wipe a tear from her eye. "You're just real cute when you get all worked up. I think your tongue was even sticking out of your mouth for a second there."

"Fuck you, Tam," I said, reaching for the first thing I could get my hand on and launched it at her. A garter belt landed on her head like some kind of sexual halo. I snickered. "That's a good look for you."

Tamsin lifted her chin. "Not the first time I've had lingerie on my head. Won't be the last."

"All hail Tamsin, Queen of the Sex Vampires."

"And don't you forget it, bitch. That shit is official now."

We shared a grin at the reminder of her position on the Council. I'd been so busy unloading all my drama on her, we hadn't gotten around to talking about any of that yet.

"So where is your sex-on-a-stick reaper?" Tamsin asked.

"What?" I asked, blinking at the sudden subject change.

"You mentioned him while chatting with Shep, and you two have been practically joined at the hip, but he's nowhere to be found, so what gives?"

"He and I . . . things got complicated after Thana killed Eli. Shep's here to let me know Graves is apparently looking for me. Although, I can't imagine he's looking very hard if he hasn't tried here yet." My voice soured toward the end.

Shep shrugged. "Look, Squid, I have nothing better to do as long as I don't have a body so I'm keeping an eye out on my best friend. He may be banging my asshole sister, but he's still my friend—and currently one in some hot water after the shit the other one pulled." He wrinkled his nose in disgust. One of the few physical reactions we both shared with things.

"The other one?"

"Bad Salem," he responded, amusement leaching from his voice entirely.

"You're really not a fan of her," I murmured.

Something flashed in his eyes. "Talk to Graves. Make up. As much as I don't like the idea of you two fucking, you could do a lot worse. You have, in fact."

My lips pressed together. I wasn't in the mood to be lectured on my dating habits.

"I'm aware."

Half his mouth curved up, but the smile didn't meet his eyes. "Fix things there. You're going to need his help."

"That all? Any other vague warnings you wanna throw my way?"

"Yeah. Either find me a body, or figure out a way to bring me back. And soon; if you can manage to stop eating long enough to do it."

With that, he disappeared. I let out a sigh.

"So," Tamsin drawled. "I see not much has changed between you two."

"Got that much from a one-sided conversation?"

"Yup," she popped the p. "He's right though, you know."

"What?"

"About Graves. I don't know what all happened, but that guy clearly cares about you—and I've never seen you this way with a guy, so I'd gamble a guess that you care an awful lot about him too." She gave me a knowing look.

"You got that much out of my responses? I didn't even say his name—"

"Your heart rate picks up when you talk about him. Your scent changes. Not to mention your other mojo that I don't really have a way to explain since you're not a succubus. Anyways—point is yes, I picked up enough to tell you that whatever happened there, kiss and make up. You got enough other shit going on to be fighting with him right now, and as much as I love catching up, being a Council member is fucking exhausting. I need a midnight snack and some shut-eye before this meeting at the butt crack of dawn tomorrow."

I tried not to think about the fact that her 'midnight snack' was probably the half-naked dude she kicked out of her room when I showed up, and I focused on the truth of what she was saying.

"You're right."

"Of course I am." She smiled sweetly.

I snorted.

"Oh, one last thing," I said before going ghost on her. "You can't tell the Council everything I've told you. If all the factions knew what I am—what I really am . . . Dom is worried that things would escalate into a real war. As it is, the shit with Gerard making an escape and Eli being dead is going to be a major problem. Act surprised when they tell you tomorrow."

Tamsin shrugged. "It won't be a problem. Unlike you, I have no issues lying. If it keeps my best friend and people safe, it's a win-win. You don't have anything to worry about here."

My smile dropped the moment I turned ghostly and zipped across Farrow's Square to reappear in the passenger seat of Graves' car.

It was dark inside. The engine was cut.

In front of us, darkness filled the void.

I recognized the spot as Widow's Peak.

The cliff named for the people that stepped off its rocky

edge and took the four-hundred-foot plunge straight down. Graves sat in the driver's seat, staring straight ahead. Dark circles lined his eyes. The strain of all that had happened was taking its toll.

I pulled myself out of the spirit realm, and he didn't even twitch.

"I've been looking for you."

Undone

"THAT'S the word on the street," I said, matching his tone and staring straight ahead.

"Gretel?" he guessed.

"Shep," I corrected. "I haven't seen Gretel after the . . . incident."

He made a soft humming sound in his throat.

Silence filled the space between us, and I shifted uncomfortably in my seat. Despite the fact that I had a tendency to annoy and frustrate Graves on a regular basis, this was the first time I actually felt guilty for upsetting him.

"Look, I'm—"

"Salem, I—"

We broke off and looked at each other with bemused grins.

"You first," he offered.

"I'm sorry things went down the way they did. Surprising you like that, and having Thana with me. I didn't think—"

"Clearly," he said, but it was soft and laced with affection.

"I'm trying to apologize, but if you want to crack jokes, I can be an asshole instead . . ."

He gestured with a hand for me to continue.

"Thana . . ." I started and broke off, blowing out a frustrated breath. "She showed me how to travel through the spirit realm—the place you and I pop in whenever we die. It's super convenient, by the way. That's how I managed—well, obviously you figured that part out," I said, rambling now. "We weren't spying on you and Randy because I'm a brat. I wanted to be there in case you needed backup, and it gave me a way to practice the whole spirit form thing. You were never even supposed to see me—us—but then Eli and the gun, and I just—"

"Salem, it's okay. I'm not upset about that."

"You're not?"

He shook his head.

"So it's the Eli thing? Look, I'm sorry. I didn't know she would do something like that, and I would have brought him back, you know I would have, but he straight up told me—"

"Salem, stop," he said, interrupting my flow of words. "I get it. I don't like it, but I get it."

"So if it's not that either, what are you mad about?"

Graves studied me, his eyes traveling over my face like a caress. "It's Thana. I just don't trust her or her motives. Granted, I don't know her well, and maybe that's part of it, but it just seems like every time she's around shit hits the fan."

"I think that's just our lives right now, Graves. Shit was a mess before she ever set foot in Farrow's Square."

He sighed. "Yeah, maybe. Things are just really delicate right now, and what Thana did put a lot of people in jeopardy. It put you in jeopardy," he said, reaching out and taking my hand.

Heat raced through my body from where we were connected, sending little goosebumps up my arms.

"I'm tougher than I look."

"You are," he agreed. "I just don't know how someone who insists they are on your side would willingly put you at risk like that. By just shooting Eli, she basically poured gasoline on a raging fire. She plays with people's lives like they are no more than pieces on a chessboard. Including yours."

I couldn't disagree with his assessment. Thana had been very clear about her feelings regarding mortals. Their lives held little value to her. But my gut was telling me she hadn't been lying when she said she was trying to help.

"She doesn't agree with keeping what I am a secret," I finally said.

"It shouldn't matter. If she truly has your back, she should respect your wishes, not try and talk you out of them. She should be trying to help you accomplish your goals, not make them blow up in your face."

We fell silent again, both of us knowing we weren't going to solve the problem that was Thana right now. And even though things might not be totally resolved, I couldn't help but feel better knowing that the reason he'd been upset was because he'd essentially been worried.

"For what it's worth, I am sorry."

"I know, me too," he said, offering me a tired half-smile.

"So does this mean we can get on to the kissing portion of the evening?" I asked with a not-so-subtle smile.

"The what?" he asked with a laugh.

"Tamsin told me we should just kiss and make up. It feels like we just checked one of those things off the list, which means . . ."

He leaned into me, his lips crashing into mine, hard and heavy. We went from zero to a hundred in a second.

I reached up, grasping the back of his neck as I twisted more to open myself up to him. Hands grabbed me by the waist.

Our kiss broke as he started to lift me. I bent my leg at an odd angle, maneuvering it past the center console and dodging the steering wheel as he pulled me onto his lap. I straddled him at the same time one of his hands fell away. The seat drew back more at an angle.

"That's better," I purred.

Graves' hands slid from my waist, past my hips, partway down my thighs.

Warm fingers pressed into my flesh. His nails bit into my skin past my thin jeans as he widened my legs further, dragging my lower body over his.

A breath hissed between my teeth.

"For a guy that never dates, you sure know your way around the female body," I groaned as he leaned up.

Kisses peppered my jaw before trailing down my neck. His teeth toyed with the skin at the base of my neck, not really biting, but hot as fuck all the same. He sucked once, and my nipples tightened.

I tried to widen my legs further and gain more friction, but the side of the door and center console stopped me.

A growl slid between my lips and he chuckled against my skin.

"Feeling needy, Salem?"

"If you don't work on finishing what you started, I'll—"

"What?" he asked, his voice was dark. Husky. "What exactly will you do, Salem?" One of the hands on my thighs curled inward. His thumb brushed up against the inside of my jeans. He slid his hand between us, slowly rubbing his palm up and down along the seam.

"More," I grunted, pressing into him.

The other hand on my hip slid upward. It curved over my ass, trailed up my back, and came to rest at the base of my skull where my head met my neck. He threaded his fingers through my hair and pulled me toward him.

Our lips met, and that fire he'd ignited turned into an all-out inferno. My skin was hot. My core ached. My head pounded with the most delicious heat.

I parted my lips, and his twined with mine. His kiss not just consuming me, but devouring me whole.

Shudders racked my body as the pleasure I sought evaded me. It was right there . . . but still too far.

"More," I moaned against his lips.

He chuckled again, and my hands turned to fists as I pulled at his hair.

"You never answered my question," he murmured. "What will you do?"

I pulled back just enough to meet his eyes.

"Come undone," I whispered.

There was no amusement in his face now. Only desire.

"I might like to see that," he whispered back. His eyes trailed over my features, glowing an ethereal blue.

I leaned forward, but instead of kissing him, I lowered my lips to his neck. My teeth trailed over his bare flesh, the scent of spearmint and aftershave calling to me.

He groaned when I sucked on a patch of skin and didn't stop.

"In case you haven't noticed, it's going to be a tight fit trying this in the car."

I pulled harder on his hair, forcing him back against the seat. The release of my lips from his skin made a popping sound.

"So we move outside the car," I said, entirely undeterred.

"For anyone that could drive by to see—"

His reply broke off as I dropped one hand from his hair and maneuvered it between our bodies to run my fingers over the bulge in his jeans. He hardened at my touch. Graves' breath turned ragged.

"Unless you were planning on leaving us both high and dry, you got a better option?" I asked softly. Seductively. At least it was my best attempt at seductive.

In response, one of his hands dropped away from me, flinging the car door open at the same time the other grasped my ass. He kicked a leg out of the door and twisted our bodies without breaking us apart, and then lifted me out of the car.

My legs went to fully wrap around his waist.

His other arm banded around my hips, pressing me firmly against him as he kicked the car door shut.

Night enveloped us. From this distance, the center of

Farrow's Square was far away from the cliff that overlooked it. Only the stars in the sky looked down on us as he set me on the back of his car. Not a soul would see us unless they were driving up here for the view.

No one would hear us, or more accurately, me.

Still, there was a certain thrill to it. The possibility of being caught out in the open, as unlikely as it was.

Graves unbuttoned my jeans and dragged the zipper down slowly.

"You sure about this?" he asked, voice thick with need. He was giving me the option to back out, but there was no way in hell that was happening now.

I flattened my hands behind me, the metal cool against my palms. I used them to brace my weight as I lifted my hips. He pulled my jeans and panties a quarter way down my thighs. I released my legs on his waist and my ass hit the trunk, but Graves didn't seem to care. He made quick work of my shoes and tossed my clothes next to me on the car.

His hands came to rest on my knees. He pulled me forward until I was only just sitting on the edge. My legs dangled over the trunk, and it was only because of the angle I was leaning and the way my hands were braced that kept me on the car entirely.

Then he dropped to his knees.

"What are you—" I didn't get to finish my question as he pulled one of my legs over his shoulder and went down on me.

His tongue whorled around my clit, giving it the love I *really* needed.

My hips jumped. The action bordering on the edge of extreme pleasure and pain.

A finger pressed against my entrance.

Slowly. Excruciatingly slow, he slid it inside me.

My toes curled, and I angled my other leg over his shoulder, then used my heels to press into his back.

Graves chuckled, the faint brush of his breath setting my skin aflame.

He licked me again, adding a second finger, and I writhed.

When his lips clamped around that sensitive bud, I thought release was at last in my grasp. But Graves being the asshole he was, sucked once, only to still his movements and wait till the heat abated enough I didn't detonate when he did it again.

"You motherfucker," I snapped, my upper body shooting up.

Lips still locked to my core, he reached up with his free hand and pressed it to my stomach, trying to push me back.

His teeth brushed against me. He sucked again, and my mouth parted. My jaw fell open as a wave of ecstasy washed over me.

"I'm not leaving you high and dry, as you put it. So chill the fuck out. I just want to hear you scream," he murmured.

And with that, a third finger entered me, and he started all over.

I leaned back, but my body coiled tight. A fine sheen of sweat covered me. My legs shook from being pushed so close to the edge again and again.

"I'm going to be screaming for a whole different reason if you don't—" The words left me as he nibbled harder. The brush of his teeth drawing a groan from me. Graves sucked my clit between his lips in long pulls, his fingers moving faster than before. Sweat slicked my back and dotted my temple as I approached that precipice. My hips jolted against him, chasing my peak and yet fighting how close I was.

Graves crooked his fingers and sucked one more time.

That was all it took.

White blinded me. My body contracted as I came violently and blacked out.

I was still shuddering around his hand when my vision cleared, the stars above that had blurred were coming back into focus as I stared up at them. I peered down my body at Graves to see an arrogant fucking grin on his face.

"If you don't fuck me," I started, breathing heavily.

"Oh, I'm fucking you," he assured me, standing up. "You don't need to worry about that. I just wanted to see you do it."

He pulled a condom from his pocket and ripped it open with his teeth.

"Do what?"

"Come undone," he replied, unzipping his jeans and pushing his boxers out of the way. He made quick work of putting the condom on and then knocked my legs aside, moving closer.

He grasped my hips and thrust once, entering me.

My body rocked into his. A delicious sigh leaving me. His mouth was good. Very good.

But I had a feeling round two with him inside me was going to be better.

I wrapped my legs around his waist as he slowly worked

in and out of me. He groaned as my hips moved in tandem with his. The car shook, bouncing with our movements.

"You're a brat," Graves said, panting hard. His eyes glowed brighter than the stars in that moment. "But you're my brat."

I whimpered, chasing my own release once more. I could tell he was pacing himself by the tic in his jaw as he worked me up again. His shaft hardened further as his movements grew erratic. Wild. Devastating.

If I didn't know better, I'd say he wanted to wreck me.

But I did know better.

He didn't just want to; he was going to.

My body was more than happy to comply. Heat filled me once more and my legs went stiff. My head lolled a bit as I arched into him. I was a receptacle of pleasure that had been drawn too tight. It bordered pain, how close I was, and how much I needed him to push me over.

"Graves," I moaned.

He was too far gone, chasing his own release to even flash me a cocky grin. Desire rode him as hard as it did me. Our eyes met, my own shuttered as my eyelids threatened to close. His pupils were blown wide, making the blue in them darker. His expression was fierce, bordering on the edge of uncontrollable. The vein in his temple throbbed.

"Come for me, Salem," he growled.

Graves thrust into me once more, our skin slapped together, and I came.

This time, it wasn't the blinding wave of a dam bursting, but instead the rocky waves washing over me. My legs tightened. I pulsed around him.

An animal-like sound escaped him.

Several moments passed where we stood there like that.

Well, he stood, I still half sat on the back of his car even though he was probably supporting more of my weight given how much of my ass he was holding. Sweaty lips pressed against my temple before he moved back, slowly supporting less of me instead of letting me fall off.

He could be sweet like that. Sometimes.

"Come on, I need to get you back before Esme gets any ideas about shooting me with a crossbow again."

I snickered, falling back against the trunk and stretching my legs out.

"She doesn't care that we're together as long as she doesn't have dumb grandchildren," I laughed.

His lips pressed together, clearly having his own thoughts about that. "I highly doubt they would be dumb. Devious maybe, but not stupid. Besides, it's a bit far out for that, but I imagine she'll get over it when we get there."

I blinked. Did he just . . .

Graves, seeming to have realized what he'd said, paled. "I know we haven't talked about what *this* is between us with everything going on, but I—"

"I love you." The words left me in a rush. "And not just because you have a magic dick, although if I'm being completely honest, I am starting to wonder if you might be related to Tamsin—"

His lips crashed into mine once more. I wound my arms around his neck, pulling him to me. My heart felt bigger, lighter, than it had in a long while.

I didn't need to hear the words to know how he felt back, but that didn't stop him from saying, "I love you too, Salem." He gave me one more peck on the lips. "Now get dressed, I meant what I said about Esme. Now that she knows I can't die, I can't imagine she won't exploit the fuck out of that if given the opportunity."

I dressed quickly, a stupid, happy smile on my face as we climbed back into the car.

"Hey, Graves," I said as he pulled off the cliffside. "We'll figure it out. When all of this is over . . . we'll figure out what comes next for us."

One corner of his mouth twitched. It was his eyes that smiled back at me as he said, "I want that."

So did I, but even with how happy I felt in the moment, it couldn't stop that dark inkling from creeping in. I wanted to figure out what forever looked like with him, but first, we had to survive long enough to get there.

Line in the Sand

REAPERS STRETCHED out along the edge of the werewolf's territory, the seven Council members standing in a small knot just in front of us. The sun was just about to complete its descent, and the sky was a deep orange with hints of purple creeping in.

Usually I loved this time of day, but all I saw as the sun sank lower in the sky was time running out.

Gerard had escaped last night. There was no one for the pack to turn over.

But only Graves and I knew that.

In the aftermath of Eli's death, Graves was worried the reapers would hunt Gerard and kill him on sight—and whoever he was with. If that happened, all hell would break loose. So he left that tidbit out when recanting his story of self-defense.

One dead body was enough to handle. While Gerard wasn't innocent, maybe things would cool down if he were removed from the situation . . .

Or so we hoped.

I let out a heavy sigh.

Beside me, Graves brushed his fingers against my arm. I knew it was his way of checking to see if I was okay. I offered him a tight smile before my eyes drifted across the smattering of houses and trees in front of me.

Unlike most supernaturals who predominantly lived scattered throughout the town, the shifters had an innate need to be surrounded by nature. So their entire community was based at the edge of the city limits and overlapping the beginning of the woods. Totally made sense when you factored in the whole shifting and running in the moonlight thing.

However, instead of being peaceful, this little standoff I was currently a part of was tense as fuck.

As the last few minutes before the deadline ticked by, more and more of the wolves came outside, standing across from us with expressions that ranged from neutral to outright hostile, and the tiny bit of hope I had slowly dwindled. This wouldn't work if they came out in a show of force. I'd been hoping with him gone that maybe they'd try to play it off . . .

Stupid. I shook my head. *Of course this wasn't going to work.*

Things had been bubbling up for a while, like a storm on the horizon. Electricity was in the air, and all we were waiting for was that first drop of rain before the sky opened and we were swept away by the tempest's fury.

The sun dipped that last inch, and I swallowed.

Time was up.

"Where's the boy, Hal?" Nocturna demanded.

"Doesn't waste any time, does she?" I muttered to Graves.

The barest shadow of a smile crossed his lips, and he shook his head once.

The werewolf named Hal took a step closer and lifted his arms in an exaggerated shrug. "Guess he had other plans tonight."

"Hal," the female wolf beside Nocturna said with a warning growl. "Don't do this."

So the werewolf head wasn't in on it? I wasn't sure if that was good or bad, given half her faction was lined up and ready to fight.

"Sorry, Serena. Can't help you this time."

The Council's female werewolf representative shook her head, her hands curling and uncurling at her sides. "I know he's your son, but you're not helping him by trying to hide him. This is your last chance. Turn Gerard over to us, and let us get this over with."

"See, that's going to be a problem. Gerard's not here."

Beside me, Sam cracked his neck and started shaking out his arms like a boxer getting ready for the bell to ring.

Nerves fluttered low in my stomach.

Ah hell. I honestly wasn't sure if our decision not to say anything was fixing to make this better or worse.

I wanted to say something to stop this. Graves took one look at my face and slowly shook his head. I blew out a frustrated breath, taking the hint.

"Tsk, tsk," the noise startled me. I glanced sideways to see Gretel standing there. My eyes widened.

"What are you doing here?" I hissed.

"Checking in on you." She shrugged. "Where's your sister?"

"Not here," I growled under my breath.

Sam looked over and gave me a funny look, then shrugged and returned his attention to the wolves.

"Oh? Showing her true colors already?" Gretel asked. "That was faster than expected."

"We need to talk, but I'm a little busy right now," I whispered as quietly as I could manage.

"You seem a little busy for everyone lately."

"Yeah, well, that's what happens when I can't go twenty-four hours without shit happening—"

"Well, if you're so *busy,* I'll make this quick. Death wants to know your answer."

"What?" I snapped under my breath.

"I didn't stutter," she said with an attitude, stepping in front of me. Her black eyebrows lifted, and she pursed her red lips.

"I have a week," I replied.

"And? They want to know if you've made up your mind."

"No." I glanced past her to see that things were heating up. "I don't have all the facts, and to get those, I need time. If Death wants me to hurry up, it should pay me a visit itself."

She scrunched her nose. "I'll relay the message. Oh, and Salem?"

I lifted an eyebrow in answer.

"They, them; pronouns. *It* is just plain rude."

She vanished in a puff of smoke, and my jaw fell open.

Did she seriously just—

Yes, she fucking did.

I growled under my breath and several reapers looked over and then nodded in approval, clearly misunderstanding given they couldn't see ghosts. Unfortunately, as much as the impending doom of everyone in Farrow's Square was important, it was slightly less important compared to the hundred or so supernaturals with firearms currently pointed both ways.

"I thought you said you had reapers patrolling the area?" Nocturna demanded, her attention currently on Dom.

Indecision warred on several Council members' faces as they glanced between the reaper and fae representative, and the she-wolf rep who was currently speaking in harsh whispers with Hal.

"I did, but that doesn't mean things don't sometimes get past," Dom said through gritted teeth.

"Get past?" she repeated. "I suppose I shouldn't be surprised given he got past you for years."

"Nocturna," Tamsin stepped in. "Are you sure it's wise to provoke—"

"Stay out of this, succubus. We all know your kind consort with *theirs*." She threw us a scathing look, clearly not a fan of us any more than she was the wolves.

Tamsin's eyes glowed a brilliant gold as she called on her power. "Remember who you're speaking to, Tinkerbell."

Nocturna's face was priceless. It seemed to shrivel in on itself, giving her supermodel features a pinched, sour expression. Given her reaction, Tinkerbell must be the faerie version of a four-letter word. Go Tamsin.

Before Nocturna could spout off her comeback, Serena

shifted, fur enveloping her tanned skin and her body contorting as it stretched and lengthened. She started growling menacingly at Hal, whose response was to do the same.

The two wolves began snarling and circling each other. Behind them, the distinct sound of dozens of guns being cocked rang out.

The reapers acted in kind, lifting their weapons and taking aim.

Shit was about to get really bad. Real fast.

I had to do something. I couldn't just stand there and watch all these people start killing each other—even if I could bring them all back after they got it out of their system.

But what could I do?

Hal, whose fur was a deep smoky gray, let out one long howl and leapt at Serena. That seemed to be the sign the others were waiting for.

Sweat trickled down my back as I watched a female were with bright green eyes start to squeeze the trigger. I didn't think; I just knew I couldn't let her take the shot. The world started to leech of color, but before I finished the transition, Tamsin's voice boomed.

"Enough!" she shouted. "Everybody just calm the fuck down."

I could feel my heartbeat slow, and knew that somehow she'd just used her compulsion on everyone in this clearing.

"Drop your weapons," Tamsin ordered in that same powerful voice.

One by one, guns started to hit the ground.

Tamsin was turning in a slow circle, pinning everybody

with her eyes, which seemed to reinforce the hold she had over us all.

"Now I know you all have your panties in a bunch, but going all Civil War part two on each other isn't going to solve a damn thing. So, here's what we are going to do. Two of our reapers will perform an unarmed sweep of the houses, to verify that Gerard is, in fact, not here. Once that has been confirmed, the Council will formally place a bounty on his head—as is our right according to the laws we all follow. Finally, anyone found having played a role in aiding and abetting his escape will be tried and sentenced according to our laws. Is that clear?"

I felt as Zen as Randy after his pregaming sessions, but it didn't dull the sense of pride I had watching my best friend handle this like the badass bitch I'd always known she was. She really did deserve that place on the Council. Not only was she powerful, but she was fair and levelheaded. Mostly.

The reapers were the first to nod, then the Council— although I could tell from the stiff way most of them were holding themselves that they did not appreciate being on the end of Tam's mass compulsion.

Finally, a few of the wolves started to nod.

"Do not make me force you to do what you know is right," she warned.

Power leached from the air and several people sagged.

I grabbed Graves' hand and dragged him over to the side, away from everyone else.

"We've got a problem," I said quietly.

"I'll say. As soon as they figure out what actually

happened, the Council's going to come after us," Graves replied.

"No—well, not that. Yes, that's a problem too, but I'm talking about our *other* problem."

Graves squinted at me. "Thana?"

"Gretel," I replied. "She paid me a visit. Death wants an answer."

"But it gave you a week."

"Yeah, that's what I said too. Apparently Death is an impatient fucker. Must be where I get it. Anyways, I need to figure out who it is in this life so I can talk to them."

"Graves. Kaine. Get your asses over here," Dom called.

I lifted my head and froze like a deer in the headlights.

How did they already find out—

"Don't talk. Let's see what he wants," Graves said under his breath. His hand pressed against my lower back, guiding me toward the group that formed around our Fuckface leader.

"You two are going to check the grounds," he said.

"But—" I started. Welp. Silence didn't last long.

Dom stepped forward and lowered his voice.

"We can't take weapons onto their territory, and I'm not losing anyone else."

Oh. Well. When he put it that way . . .

"We can make the rounds," Graves said.

"Good. Try not to die . . . again."

Somehow that was almost endearing coming from him.

We walked across the clearing and past the Council. Tamsin met my gaze and nodded once. She approved of them sending me, not that anyone outside of the reapers and herself knew why.

The line of shifters parted. We were just at the tree line when Dom called out.

"Report back to Gamma Rho when you're done. Alexander wants to see you both."

Oh goody. More secrets coming to light.

Considering all the ones already on my plate, I wasn't exactly thrilled.

"Come on," Graves said, pulling me into the woods. "Let's get this over with."

Reborn

"WELL, that was a fucking waste of time," I muttered, wiping dirty hands on my jeans.

"It was a formality that allowed the Council—" Graves started, catching up with me as we walked up to Gamma Rho.

"I see your lips moving, but all I hear is blah blah Council bullshit blah."

His lips twitched. "That was actually the gist of it."

I pressed my lips together and nodded. "Thought so."

We reached the back door, and Graves held it open for me, grasping my wrist and holding me in place so he could duck down and give me a kiss. It was over as fast as it began, but the brief slide of his lips against mine was enough to set my blood on fire.

"What was that for?" I asked, a little dazed as we moved into the kitchen.

He shrugged. "Do I need a reason?"

"Nope, definitely not. Feel free to do that as often as you like. Ideally when we're alone and can get naked."

For a second there, I forgot where we were, and Dom's low whistle had my cheeks burning as reality came crashing back.

"It's amazing you two ever manage to get anything done," he said with a shake of his head.

"Yeah, well, I'm an amazing multitasker," I said dryly. *No matter what Esme says.*

The purposeful lift of his eyebrows told me exactly what he thought of that, so I let my finger do the talking.

Dom chuckled. "Alexander is waiting for you upstairs."

Graves waved at him in thanks and started leading the way. We'd already called ahead and reported in, so Dom and the Council both knew what we'd uncovered during our search. Namely, not a damn thing.

We made our way quickly up the first flight of stairs and down the hall. Graves opened the door at the end and a shiver raced down my spine.

"Cold?" he asked.

I shook my head. The last time we were up here we died, and Shep the sheep ended up being bar-b-que. Not my favorite memory.

My face must have shared the direction of my thoughts because Graves reached back and grabbed my hand, squeezing it tightly as we walked up the second flight of stairs.

"We have some good memories up here too," Graves said. A dark thrum to his voice as he gestured to the wall he'd pinned me against.

My lips curled up. "True."

We shared a heated look, but he knocked once on the reaper door before twisting the knob and pushing it open.

"Dad?"

Alexander was leaning against the mantel, staring into the flames below. It was so similar to what James had been doing that the two images transposed over each other for a second before I blinked them away and stepped inside.

Alexander turned and gave us a smile that didn't reach his eyes. "I appreciate you both making some time to come and see me. I'm sorry I had to put this off this long. With the changes on the Council . . ." He shook his head, clearly not really wanting to go into it.

I shrugged. "No problem. We needed to see you anyway. Turns out, I'm not the only member of the lady death club anymore."

Graves' eyebrows flew up. He thought I was talking about Thana.

Alexander's expression was almost identical to his son's. "What do you mean?"

"My aunt, Esme. When I brought her back, I triggered the reaper gene. She's one of you guys." I shrugged again. "I wasn't sure how well-received she would be, so I figured I would tell you first and see what you thought."

"Interesting," Alexander said, running his fingers over his lips. "I wonder how many other sisters and daughters carry the gene."

"My guess? All of them."

Alexander was nodding. "Would have been helpful to know that years ago. We could have bolstered our numbers. Maybe then we wouldn't be in this predicament."

Fat chance.

"Gamma Rho are misogynists. You guys couldn't have handled people like my aunt kicking your asses," I quipped.

Graves gave me a look, and I shrugged. What was Alexander going to do?

Shit. That's what.

To both our surprise, though, Daddy Graves let out a low chuckle.

"Yes, I suppose there is that. Still, maybe things would have turned out differently, had the reapers not gone down the path they have. I fear for our longevity in the coming war."

"War?" I repeated. "But—"

"It's inevitable, Salem. Dominick is doing his best to hold it off, but the Council wants blood. The supernaturals of Farrow's Square are tired of death. I saw the writing on the wall as well as anyone, but I was too stupid to do anything about it. I deserved to be stripped of my title. But that's not why I called you here."

He turned around from the fireplace and crossed his hands behind his back. Strong blue eyes settled on me. I had to try not to fidget under his stare.

"Why did you call me here, then?"

"You're being hunted," he said simply.

My lips parted. *How could he possibly know—*

"By a monster. The legends don't give it a name, but the outcome is clear every time."

"You're going to need to start over," I said slowly.

He nodded. "Right, of course. Since the beginning of the reapers' existence, you, or some version of you, has popped up once every few generations—often in times of strife. Trouble follows you, Salem, but you probably already know that by now."

His lips quirked up, but I wasn't so amused.

"I didn't know why before. None of us have. It's only now, in this life, that you've shown us who and what you are."

"How do you know it was me? In all these lives?"

"You look the same," he said. "But you're also always a twin, and it's always fraternal. Each time you're born, chaos ensues during the years you grow. Whatever is hunting you rips apart our ranks every time. It devastates the supernatural community. That's why we came to Farrow's Square to begin with. At first, we thought the monster was after us. It's only once we got here that we realized what draws it is *you*."

He didn't know. Not everything at least, but he knew enough. Which made me wonder . . .

"Did my father know this?"

"Yes, but most do not. It's a piece of information that's been passed from one reaper head to the next."

"If you knew she was being hunted, why did you agree to the blood rite?" Graves asked.

Alexander smiled. "If I tried to separate you two, it would have gone poorly. You would have fought even harder. While she dies in every life, she also comes back. I figured whatever was hunting her would find her, and inevitably you as well . . ."

"You thought the blood rite would bring me back with her," Graves said.

Alexander looked away. Not embarrassed, not reproachful, but still aware of the deadly game he was playing.

"It was a long shot," Graves' father said. "But chaos was already emerging. The tensions were building once more. I didn't know how to save you—but I thought maybe if you both died, you'd both come back."

"Well, so far that's the case," I said. "So your gamble seems to have paid off."

Graves didn't say anything as he stared at his dad, clearly having a hard time coming to terms with this.

"With the way things are going, I have reason to believe the monster has found you in this life," Alexander said at last, looking away from his son.

"It has," I replied.

He blinked, turning to me. Clearly, he didn't expect that.

"You know about it?"

"Recently we've had some run-ins." I shrugged. "The thing hunting us can be killed . . . in a way. I don't know how, though."

Only one person does . . .

Thana.

It all came back to fucking Thana.

On one hand, she'd broken that tenuous trust between us. On the other hand, Alexander's story checked out. It made more sense than even he knew.

A thought occurred to me.

"Am I the reason no one can leave Farrow's Square?"

Alexander tilted his head. A begrudging, "Yes," slid from his lips. "You're always born of a reaper line. In the past, we tried to . . . offset the consequences by handling you ourselves early on."

"You mean you kill her?"

"We tried to," Alexander corrected. "But we can't. Not

even splitting her soul works. It just pieces itself back together."

"You bastard—" Graves growled.

"*I* haven't done anything. The last time that was attempted was over a hundred years ago. After we realized that wouldn't work and that nothing will stop the creature from finding her, we decided it was best to watch and keep an eye on her. See if we can figure out what it is that draws the monster. At the very least, confining her to Farrow's Square meant this thing wasn't out killing whatever humans might surround her."

"You knew what I was when you took over after my father died, then," I said.

Alexander nodded. "I had hoped that you wouldn't come back, and that at least in this life . . . well, you know."

"But she did come back," Graves said.

"She did," Alexander nodded. "And there will be war because of it."

Unless I could kill Death.

Or Thana.

Confrontation

I SAT IN THE IMPALA, drumming my fingers on the steering wheel as I stared at the door to my house. I'd left Graves at Gamma Rho, knowing that the coming confrontation needed to happen alone.

"Can't avoid this forever, Salem," I muttered, climbing out of the car.

I may not be happy with my soul sister right now—understatement, I was fucking furious with her—but all roads led to Thana. It had become clear to me that she was at the heart of this. Thana was the key . . . but to what?

My thoughts continued to chase each other as I pushed open the door and tossed my purse down on the little table beside it.

"Salem, honey, is that you?" Esme called from the living room.

"Yeah," I half-heartedly hollered.

"Can you come here for a minute?"

I sighed, not sure I had it in me to deal with Esme's

antics right now, but also too curious to find a reason not to.

I went off in the direction of her voice, my thoughts still focused on Thana when a loud crash sent my pulse racing.

Oh fuck, Esme, what did you do this time?

On high alert now, I jogged the rest of the way, coming to a dead stop when I found Esme preening in the living room. Her arms were crossed, and a smug grin was stretched across her face beneath her ghost goggles. Beside her, Aurora was hurling books across the room from the shelves lining the wall. The girl was throwing a proper ghostly temper tantrum if I'd ever seen one.

Not that I could blame her. As far as I could tell, she was tethered to a metallic box that was flung open beneath her, a soft pink light glowing from inside of it as well as from some kind of arcane markings on the side. I wasn't sure what the box had been before Esme repurposed it, but it almost looked like a jack-in-the-box without the creepy clown. I was guessing this was Esme's ghost trap, but I didn't have the slightest clue how it worked.

"Esme," I said slowly. "What did you do?"

"What's it look like?"

"Like you caught a ghost," I muttered, still not believing it.

Esme's smile grew wider. "Right in one!"

"You get me out of here. Right. Now," Aurora demanded, sending more books flying.

"How did you even manage this?" I asked, my eyes darting between the two of them.

"I had all the equipment. I was just missing the secret ingredient."

"The secret ingredient," I repeated.

She nodded. "When I explained to Richard what I was trying to do, he was more than helpful."

"Richard . . . your fuck buddy?"

Esme's eyes sparkled. "Fuck buddy and high warlock."

Of course. Of fucking course Esme was banging a warlock.

"So Richard gave you this magic ingredient, and now your ghost trap works?"

She gestured to a furious Aurora. "Obviously."

Fuck me. Esme shouldn't be left alone. Although . . . my aunt definitely knew how to get things done. Who else would have managed something like this?

Maybe I should recruit her help more often.

"I can't believe you fell for it," I said to Aurora, which clearly was not the right thing to say.

"What do you mean 'fell for it'?" she screeched. "I was just over here minding my own business and this reaper bitch sucked me into the living realm. As if she had the right to summon one of Death's messengers!"

The sheer fury in Aurora's voice gave me pause. This was no teenage meltdown.

"Esme . . . do you know how long that trap will hold?"

"Until I release it."

"Good, we're about to put it to the test."

"What?" Aurora shrieked. "Salem Kaine, if you don't let me go right now—"

"You'll what? Haunt me? You already spied on me and Graves. Seems like this is fair payback as far as I can tell. If this doesn't teach you to stop spying on people . . ."

She scowled at me, her arms crossed over her chest. "If you think I'm about to agree to anything you say—"

"You will," I said, perfectly confident. "Because if you don't, you'll be stuck here indefinitely."

Hatred shone in her eyes. "And to think I actually liked you."

I rubbed at my chest, giving her a fake frown. "Ouch, that hurts."

"Just tell me what you want," she spat.

"I want to talk to your boss."

"Excuse me?"

Esme lifted her eyebrows, but remained uncharacteristically silent.

"You heard me."

"You . . . want to talk to Death? You were serious about that?" she asked, some of her fury subsiding. She cocked her head and crossed her arms over her chest.

"I take it Gretel actually relayed my message?"

Aurora shrugged. "She might have mentioned it to them. Why do you want to talk to Death?"

"Because I want to know why they want Thana dead— and how to do it."

Silence expanded between us before Aurora threw her head back and let out a bubbling laugh. A tub of popcorn appeared out of nowhere and she tossed a few pieces in her mouth.

"You? Kill Thana?" She shook her head, tears streaming out of her eyes from laughing so hard. "You're too soft. Too human. You don't have it in you."

I narrowed my eyes.

"She's got a point," Esme said.

"Seriously?" I turned on my aunt.

She merely shrugged. "It's not a bad thing, per se. You're just better suited for getting into trouble—not cleaning it up."

I shook my head. "I cannot believe you right now."

"Where's Death?" Esme asked the ghost.

Aurora pursed her lips. "As if I'd tell you."

Esme grinned. "I was hoping you'd say that."

She lifted her gun, and Aurora snorted. "I'm already dead. That can't do anything to me."

"Before I had it adjusted, probably not. But now . . ." My aunt smiled, and even I was creeped the fuck out.

Instead of fear, Aurora's eyes narrowed. Her popcorn disappeared as if the kid gloves were coming off. "You wouldn't."

A shot rang out.

Fury flashed through Aurora's features. "You—you—bitch!"

A black sickly substance drained from the hole in her chest where Esme had shot her. My aunt grinned. "I've been called worse things, dearie. Keep talking or the next one goes in your head."

"You can't kill me," Aurora insisted. "I'm already dead."

"While that may be true, you don't seem to enjoy getting shot." Esme shrugged. "Your choice. Tell us where Death is, or stay trapped in here."

Aurora grumbled under her breath.

"We can't hear youuuu," Esme called out in a sing-song voice. The barrel of her pistol lifted to Aurora's head.

"Death is everywhere and nowhere. They exist in every realm."

"That's not a real answer," I said. "You're delaying."

"As are you," Aurora shot back. "You haven't made up your mind about Thana. Not truly. The abomination still walks the Earth and the realm of spirits because you won't do what needs to be done."

"You call her an abomination, but what's her crime? Existing. She may not be a good person, but—"

"You make excuses for her even when the truth looks you in the eye. Thana isn't simply a bad person. She's the worst. She's convinced Death is the monster—but answer me this, Salem. If Death wanted you dead, why have they waited so long? If they were hunting you and had found you, why not just be done with it? Why ask for the abomination at all?"

"I—it—"

Her eyes hardened. "Ask Thana how the Black Plague was started."

When I looked in her eyes then, I saw something I never noticed before.

Something old. Something ancient.

Cold crept through my veins and I shivered as the truth hit me in the face as hard as a slap, because I knew right then—I'd been staring at Death all along.

Death *was* them. All of them.

"Death is everywhere and nowhere. *They* exist in every realm," I whispered back.

A cold smile curled her lips. "Very good, Daughter."

Pink light exploded up out of the box on the floor, practically blinding me.

The house shook. Esme stumbled.

By the time we both recovered, Aurora was gone.

"No," Esme wailed, holding up shattered metal pieces that used to be part of her trap.

"Guess she didn't want you to be able to do that again."

"Clearly," Esme said with a sigh, tossing the metal shards onto the couch. "So what do we do now?"

"Fuck if I know," I muttered, but plans were already forming in my mind.

This whole time, Death had been watching me. Keeping tabs on me. Biding their time before revealing who they really were.

This was another test; to see what I'd do and where my head was at. My anger spiked. I was tired of being a pawn in everyone else's games.

Just once it would be great if I was the one pulling the strings and in control of my own life.

But maybe, just maybe, there was a way.

If Death refused to talk, I knew someone that would.

"Thana!" I shouted.

"You're too late," the voice beside me said, but it wasn't Esme, nor was it Thana.

It was Shepard.

I turned toward my brother. Pity reflected on his ghostly features.

"What are you talking about?" I asked quietly. Dread twisted my stomach into knots. I didn't know what she'd done, but judging by the expression on his face, I knew it was bad.

"She got tired of waiting for you to give her an answer," he said. "She decided to make the choice easier for you."

"Easier?" I repeated. "Easier how?" A hard edge entered my tone. I didn't like the sound of that.

My answer came in the form of pain.

It erupted from my chest. I looked down.

Blood saturated my shirt. My knees wobbled, then collapsed as pain so intense it was blinding settled over me.

Arms grabbed my upper body. I blinked rapidly, trying to clear the spots from my vision.

"Stay with me, Salem," my aunt said, her voice calm.

"What happened?" I rasped. The last thing I saw before true darkness took me was my brother's gray eyes, his expression grim.

"War," he whispered.

Havoc

I opened my eyes and the world was washed in gray.

"Goddamnit!" I snapped. Shepard's form stood in front of me. "Where's Graves?"

My brother inclined his head, jutting his chin toward my left shoulder.

I turned. "Who killed you?" I demanded.

"Thana," he spat my soul sister's name like a curse.

I wish I could say I was surprised, but that would be a lie. If anything, part of me was just a little sad that the nagging voice in the back of my mind had been right. I wanted to trust her, but I knew she was bad news from the moment she stepped into the graveyard.

"How?" I asked. "Why?" The questions poured from my lips. I needed answers.

"She showed up at the Grimm house leading the other supes. They had Gerard in tow. Or, well, his head." Graves looked away. "Her hair was dyed pink."

That bitch.

"She's pretending to be me."

Graves nodded.

Shepard sighed. "You were given a week and time is running out. Thana tried to convince you, and after killing Eli, she realized you were too stubborn. She felt you needed motivation."

"What the fuck does that even mean?"

"You care," my brother said, coming to stand next to Graves and me. Or, well, float. "Too much, in her opinion. She went and found Gerard and brought him back. Dropped him at the feet of the Council and claimed the reapers were hiding him. The wolves were furious because they felt betrayed. The rest of the supes were angry because they felt lied to. They marched on Gamma Rho, and as far as the reapers were concerned, you were leading the charge."

"Fuck." I put my head in my hands. "I've gotta stop her—"

"Wait," both Graves and Shepard said.

Without listening, I focused on the Gamma Rho house and it appeared before me.

I shuddered. Flames consumed the frat house. Windows were smashed. Bodies littered the ground. Cops were storming the scene. Screams merged with the roar of fire.

Havoc. It was complete and utter havoc.

And there, right in the middle of it, stood my doppelgänger. Her hands behind her back, metal handcuffs glinting on her wrists.

Two reapers were leading her toward the cop car beside me.

Thana looked up, and then she smiled.

"You fucking bitch," I hissed, hoping she could

hear me.

The glint in her eye told me it didn't matter if she could. She already thought she'd won. She'd played me.

Graves moved closer, trying to soothe me with his presence. But I was beyond being soothed.

"Salem," Shepard said in a warning tone.

"Don't."

"I recognize that look. Now's not the time to go off the deep end."

"Now is *exactly* the time to go off the deep end. Thana just started a fucking war and made me out to be its ringleader. And for what? To convince me to spare her? All she did was paint a target on her back."

"She's trying to separate you from the things—the people—that matter to you. She wants to prove that in the end, she's the only constant in your life," Shepard said quietly.

I turned away from the flames and faced my twin. "She's wrong." My eyes shifted from Shep to Graves. "That might have been true once, but not anymore. Thana killed Graves thinking that the proof of his mortality would help me get over him. She'd said as much to me before. What she didn't count on was the blood rite. Graves is no more mortal than I am."

Graves and I stared at each other, sharing a look so intense it consumed me. After everything we'd been through, Graves and I were bound more tightly than Thana could ever hope to be. She might have been born from a piece of my soul, but any claim she had to me went up in flames with the Gamma Rho house.

Shepard cleared his throat. "As touching as it is to watch

you two eye-fuck each other, I'm pretty sure we have bigger problems right now."

I let out a crazed laugh. "You think?"

My twin sighed. "Salem, you need to find me a body."

I blinked at him incredulously. "You really think after all of this"—I threw my hand toward the destruction behind me—"that you coming back to life is my number one priority? I need to clear my name. I have to try and undo—"

"Salem," Shepard started in a voice so serious it stemmed my flow of words. "The dead cannot interfere."

I rolled my eyes. "So you keep saying, not that Death seems to play by their own rules."

"No, Salem. The *dead* cannot interfere."

"Repeating yourself isn't going to push you up the to-do list, Shepard. Stop being so fucking selfish."

He threw his hands up in the air and spun to Graves. "Please talk some sense into my pig-headed sister. I'll be around when you finally figure it out." With that, Shepard vanished, leaving Graves and me alone in the spirit realm.

"What do you want to do now?" he asked gently. "When we come back, we'll be in two separate places, and you'll be public enemy number one. I'm not going to be able to shield you from this. We need a game plan."

I released a pained breath from my chest.

"We need to find a way to trap Thana. If I can't take her out of the equation, I'll never be able to do damage control."

Graves nodded. "Alright, how do you plan to trap someone that can literally walk between Earth and whatever this is?"

"The in-between," I supplied.

"Right."

I turned, staring at the flames. I had no idea how many people had died or if they had bodies at all anymore. I really did need to find out how to bring someone from the in-between back to life. There had to be a way. If Thana thought Death was controlling the ghosts and managed to bring them to life when they've been dead for hundreds of years, there was a way to bring people out of the in-between. I just had to find it.

Unfortunately for all the supernaturals that had died today, I had no idea how.

What I did know was that somehow my aunt had managed to trap a ghost—which was actually Death.

Maybe there was a way to trap gods, or at least demigods.

"I need to talk to Esme," I said. "I think she can help."

"Okay." He nodded. "What then? If Thana breaks out before you have a chance to trap her, they're going to come to your house. You need a place to lie low."

"I could stay with Tamsin."

"Too obvious."

Ugh. He wasn't wrong.

"What about your place?" I asked.

Graves hesitated. "It's not that I don't want you to . . ." he started. Hurt flashed through me in the form of anger.

"Well where the fuck can I go if not Tamsin's or your place? We don't have enough time, and I can't spend it hiding in the in-between while we try to figure out what to do."

"Look, I want you to come to my place, but there are

really big odds they'll look there after the mansion and Tamsin's. Especially when they learn I didn't actually die after being mauled to death by werewolves."

I pressed my lips together. "Did you die in front of Thana?"

He nodded.

"Fuck," I cursed. "You need to lie low too, then. She's going to know something is up if you come back without a scratch on you. We need to disappear."

"Getting me out of here without being seen won't be easy . . ." He trailed off. "My body's in the house."

"The house currently on fire?"

He nodded.

Double fuck.

"Then I need to call Tamsin. She can use her succubus mojo to help get you out of here. We'll meet up at the grave-yard in case Thana decides to make a run for it sooner rather than later."

"Alright," Graves agreed. "But Salem—you need to be careful. We didn't die this time, but Thana and Death both know how to kill us for real."

I nodded. "Yeah, I need to figure out how to do that, and quickly. Before anyone else dies." With one last look at the flames, I said, "See you on the other side."

Graves' lips touched my temple before I disappeared.

My body sat on the ground of the mansion, Esme beside it. She was poking me with a broad range of objects, not seeming all that worried that her niece was dead.

I shook my head.

At least some things were still the same. Can't say I ever thought I'd love my aunt's weird-ass quirks.

I leaned over and touched my cheek.

In the blink of an eye, I went from standing over myself to gasping as I came back to life.

"Ah ha!" Esme called. "Just as I predicted!"

"What?" I asked, pushing myself to a seated position.

Esme grinned at me. "I was testing out a few of my more obscure ghost detectors. I figured if I found the right tool, I'd be able to predict the exact moment your soul returned to your body."

"By poking me?"

My aunt nodded. "This last one started to vibrate when I placed it against your skin and then not even a second later your eyes opened."

I raised an eyebrow at her. "How exactly is that helpful?"

Esme shrugged. "I don't know yet, but you have to admit, it's fascinating."

I shook my head and wrapped my arms around her, giving her a tight hug. If she was surprised by the unexpected embrace, she didn't show it. Esme squeezed me back and patted my head.

"Never change, Aunt Esme."

She chuckled and pulled back to look at my face, brushing some hair off of my forehead. "I don't think I'd know how to. Now, tell me what happened."

Anger surged, wiping out everything else. "Thana happened."

Esme's lips dipped into a frown, and her eyes went cold. It was the same look she got whenever she picked up her machete. I was starting to recognize it as Esme's 'cut-a-bitch' look. "What did she do?"

"More than I can explain right now. We don't have much time. Esme, do you think we could fix your ghost trap?"

She looked thoughtful. "I don't think so. The structure is no longer intact, and while I could weld it, the enchantment in the metal was likely lost. But," she added before I could let out the string of curses building inside me, "Richard mentioned that the device doesn't matter as much as the enchantments themselves."

"So we don't need a box?" I asked, trying not to get my hopes up. So much was riding on this plan working.

Esme shook her head. "No. Technically any object would do. Hell," she broke off with a laugh, "even a room could act as the trap, as long as the magic was in place."

I glanced around the living room, a dark smile curling my lips. "Esme . . . call Richard. Tell him to bring his magic kit—or whatever it is he needs to make one of these traps."

Esme matched my smile. "On it."

"Oh, and Esme?"

"Yes, dear?"

"Tell him we're not trying to trap a ghost this time. So make sure he brings something strong enough to trap an immortal."

It was impossible to miss the excited sparkle in my aunt's eyes. She lived for this kind of thing. Monster hunts. Supernatural fights. As long as she got to carry a weapon, she was down, no questions asked. It wasn't lost on me that she was more cut out for this life than I was.

Who knew crazy Aunt Esme would turn out to be my greatest asset?

Fuck Up

ON THE THIRD RING, Tamsin picked up.

"I need your help," I said, before she could even get a word in.

Sirens and screaming echoed through the speaker on the phone. Tamsin was uncharacteristically silent.

"Tam?" I asked, worry bubbling up. What if something happened to her—

"Yeah, I heard you." Her voice sounded thick. Raw. Emotion coated her tone, but it didn't sound like worry. It sounded like . . .

"Are you okay?" I asked slowly. Across the room, Esme was speaking in low whispers, but the sexual purr of her voice made me nauseous. *For fuck's sake, Esme.*

"You fucked up, Salem," my best friend said. A non-answer if there ever was one.

Message received. She was far from okay.

"It wasn't me. I know she looks like me and probably found a way to sound like me, but—"

"You think I don't know that?" Tamsin hissed. "You've

been my best friend since we were kids. I know she wasn't you. It doesn't change what happened here. My mom is dead, Salem."

I nearly dropped the phone.

My heart pounded. My fingers felt cold.

I'd dealt with enough loss that Sarah Cunningham's death didn't really hit me. It was my empathy for Tam's situation that did. I knew what it was like to lose a parent. I'd never wish that on her. Not in a million years.

"I can try to bring her back," I said quickly. "There might be a way—"

"But you don't know, do you?" she asked.

My silence spoke volumes.

"I know there is *a* way. We just have to find—"

"This never would have happened to begin with if you'd just told the Council what you were and who she was. Everyone hates you now, Salem. The reapers, the wolves, even the succubi think you played us—and I can't tell them what happened here because of your stupid fucking secrets. My mom is dead because of you."

Anger. So much anger.

And it wasn't undeserved.

I swallowed thickly. Wishing I had a way to make this better.

I had to find a way to fix this before Death and Thana tore my whole life apart at the seams.

"I'll find a way," I whispered.

She laughed, but it was a hollow, bitter sound. "I hope so, because if not . . .we're the ones that will pay the price."

Her words were like the cut of a knife. Each one

inflaming my guilt over how I'd handled the situation, and my anger toward Thana and Death for causing it.

"I'm sorry," I whispered into the phone line.

"Sorry doesn't make it better," my best friend replied.

Nothing was going to fix this thing between us until I found a way to bring her mom back and repair what I'd broken to begin with.

"Look, I hate to ask this, but I do need your help."

The sound of muffled cries, shouts of vengeance, and general crisis filled the gap where silence should be.

"What is it?" she asked eventually.

I lost a breath. "Graves died in Gamma Rho. His body is in the fire. When he gets out, he's going to need a diversion to cover him escaping."

"You really think I care if your fuck buddy—"

"Thana doesn't know about the blood rite, and we're trying to keep it that way. Not to mention, every time he dies—so do I. I know you're pissed at me—"

"Pissed does not even cover what I'm feeling right now, Salem."

"*I know*," I breathed. "If anyone understands that, it's me. But I need you, Tam. You can be angry. You can hate me. When this is all over, if you never want to talk to me again then so be it, but I *have* to fix this. You're right. I fucked up with how I handled Thana. Give me a chance to unfuck it."

I sensed her indecision. In the end though, I knew she would help me.

"I'll get him out of here, but after that, you're on your own until you fix this."

"Thank you—"

The line went dead before I could even finish.

Fuck. I hung my head.

I felt nauseous, the guilt and anger twisting up my insides and making me shake.

Thana's plan had been brilliant. But it only worked because of the choices I had made. As much as I wanted to pin all the blame on her, I couldn't. She never would have been able to do what she did if I had just revealed her presence. Sarah's death was on me.

All those reapers trapped in the house . . . I might as well have lit the match.

It was on me. All of it.

My anger bubbled, igniting me with its heat. I could feel the flush racing along my skin, like the first signs of a sunburn after a long summer day in the pool.

"Salem, honey? You're burning up."

I turned to Esme. "I'm fine."

"No, Salem." She pointed. "You're burning up."

Looking down, I realized the sting I'd mistaken as physical side effects of my anger was in fact actual burn marks forming on my hands and arms. As I watched, pain ratcheted up my right arm and long angry cuts formed along the already red and blistered skin. My hand began to throb, dozens of smaller cuts appearing over my knuckles. It felt like I'd punched a wall . . . or Graves had punched through a window. At least his escape seemed to be going well.

"It's Graves. I'll be okay in a minute."

Esme frowned, not looking convinced. "The boy already got himself killed once. Is he going for round two?"

"Escaping, actually."

She hummed. "At least let me get the first-aid kit. Those burns look nasty."

I nodded woodenly, Tamsin's words still replaying loudly in my mind. I needed to do something—anything—to make this better. "Esme, what did Richard say? How fast can he get here?"

She hesitated just inside the doorway before turning and giving me an apologetic smile. "He said he's going to need time to gather what we need. The kind of ingredients required, they aren't the kind he can acquire without raising suspicion."

I squeezed my eyes closed. *Perfect.*

My only solution to this shitshow was officially on pause, and there wasn't a fucking thing I could do about it.

I wanted to scream, rage, break everything around me. Instead, all I did was open my eyes and give Esme a nod.

"Be right back," she said, rushing out to gather the medical supplies.

My body ached, but I barely registered the pain.

No matter what I did, or what I tried to do, I failed. Everything I'd done the last few days had been to prevent the war and protect the people I love, and it had backfired. Spectacularly. Things couldn't have gone worse.

"Now's not the time for a pity party."

"Fuck off, Shep."

"Salem, you can't give up now. Too many people need you."

This was not what I needed to hear right now. "Maybe they'd be better off without me. I mean, at best, I have a half-formed plan to trap Thana, but even then I don't know what to do with her when I get her here. She's a demigod, and I still haven't learned how to kill an immortal. I'm no closer to figuring out how to bring souls back without a body to put them into, which means I can't help you or any of the others Thana killed today. And don't get me started on—"

"Salem, relax. Take it one step at a time."

"What are you even doing here? I thought I was too pig-headed to be around right now."

Shepard came closer, his eyes so filled with sympathy that I couldn't bear to look at them. "You're my twin, Squid, and you're hurting. I could never leave you alone at a time like this."

"I fucked everything up, Shep." My voice cracked as I spoke, betraying the emotion I was trying so hard to keep contained. It felt like if I gave into it even a little, I'd break entirely.

"No, Salem. Thana used you. These lives, they are on her. You will find a way to fix this."

"Oh yeah?" I laughed incredulously. "How?"

"Think, Salem. Think about what you need."

I threw my hands up in the air. "I need a fucking miracle, Shep."

"Alright," he nodded, "and who performs miracles?"

"I don't exactly have God on speed dial, so unless you have something useful to add . . ."

"Salem. Didn't you say that you're basically a goddess now?"

My mouth snapped shut, and I stared at my twin. He was trying to tell me something. I could sense the answer to whatever riddle he was posing like it was on the tip of my tongue.

"Yes, but I'm nowhere near powerful enough—"

"So get powerful enough."

I wanted to smack myself when it clicked. This whole time I knew what I needed to do to level up, I just hadn't pursued it because Graves asked me not to and I seemed to die fairly often as it was.

"The more I die, the more I level up . . ." I said slowly. "Maybe one of those level-ups comes with something that can fix this."

The corner of my brother's mouth curved upward. "Only one way to find out."

I looked from him to Esme, who'd just come back in waving the first-aid kit. "I have a favor to ask."

"Hm?" she asked, setting down the kit and pulling one of her machetes out of some hidden compartment in her cargo pants. She was inspecting the edge very meaningfully.

"I need you to kill me. A lot."

Death Montage

A CAR DOOR SLAMMED SHUT. The burns on my skin made me hiss as I jumped to my feet and stumbled toward the door. I'd stopped burning all of twenty minutes ago, and since then, my own advanced healing had kicked in and dealt with the worst of the damage.

The door opened right as I reached it.

Graves fell forward. His clothes were burned in most places. Red, patchy skin peeked out from what was left of it.

He grabbed the doorframe with one hand to steady himself, clearly struggling.

That was good. It would make it easier for what was to come if he wasn't top-notch.

Not that I told him that.

Just past his shoulder, a car idled in the circle driveway. Tamsin sat at the wheel. Her eyes were red, bloodshot, and sort of puffy. She stared at me, but it wasn't my best friend looking out. It was despair and grief.

Our eyes met.

Her lips formed the words, "Fix this."

"I will," I whispered back.

She nodded and pulled out of the driveaway.

I never doubted that she was serious when she said she wasn't helping me after this, but that didn't ease the pain in my chest watching her drive away.

I used that pain; let it motivate me for what was to come.

Wrapping a hand around Graves' waist, we leaned into each other as we pulled away from the front door. The toe of my boot hit the corner, and it swung shut behind us.

I turned to face Esme and ghost Shep. They stood on either side of the wooden chair. Beside it, on the dining table, an assortment of instruments were laid out, from knives to guns to poison and even a scythe.

My aunt took the business of killing me very seriously. I was beginning to wonder if she went into the wrong profession.

"What's this?" Graves asked, trying to pull away.

"A solution," I answered.

"To what exactly?" he rasped. The smoke must have fucked with his lungs some.

"We need to find a way to get rid of Death and Thana. I can't do that right now, and I can't bring anybody back this way either, not without a fresh body around . . ." I didn't look away when he started to glare. "We need a miracle, and my death mojo is the best we got. Maybe if I die enough times, I'll be able to do something to fix this."

"Or you could just be wasting time that we need to find a place to hide out for when Thana breaks out—"

"She's going to do that either way. The supes are coming for me either way. Death is coming *either way*. We tried to run from this, to prevent it—but all that's done for us so far is make things worse. I *need* to fix this, Graves. You can either help me or not, but there's no running."

Graves stared at me for a moment and then nodded. "Okay, we do this your way."

I didn't even get to respond before a shotgun went off.

There was no moment of darkness claiming me. No drifting. No cold embrace.

One minute we stood there staring at each other.

The next we popped up in our ghostly forms.

Meanwhile, my aunt stood off to the side, cocking her shotgun once more as she muttered something about us talking too much.

"She's not wrong," Shep murmured.

I gave him the finger and leaned over my body, giving Graves a quick smile. "You ready for this, Stranger Danger?"

He waved for me to go ahead. "After you."

"I can't promise she's not going to enjoy this."

Graves raised a brow. "You think?"

With that, I touched my hand and pulled us back into living color.

Esme was ready for us, this time swinging her scythe. My head was rolling across the living room floor like a hairy bowling ball before I even realized what happened.

I rubbed my throat, wincing at the sight. "Jesus, Esme."

"Maybe you need to give her the preheating-the-oven speech," Graves murmured, appearing beside me, his eyes trained on his own head.

"At least she's effective," I offered, proud of myself for hesitating only half a second before going back.

Machete, throwing knives, crossbow—that one she saved for Graves—one after the other, Esme worked through her pile of weapons, the mix of our blood splashing across her coveralls.

"Anyone else hearing Jock Jams playing in the background right now?" Shepard asked, looking far too amused as Graves and I popped back into the spirit realm.

I glared at him.

"I think your aunt missed her calling . . ." Graves said.

"I was thinking the same thing earlier. Fuck being a reaper. Esme is a damn assassin. What is with all these one-shots? I mean, I know this is what I asked her to do, but man . . . I feel like even if we were trying to fight back, we wouldn't stand a chance."

Shepard smirked. "Guess that just means you need to keep on going until you do."

I groaned. He was probably right.

I brought us back, eyes already squeezing shut in anticipation.

"What took so long that time?" Esme asked, cocking her head.

I peeked one eye open. "Just chatting with Shep—"

That's all she let me say before she threw an ax that lodged itself dead center in my forehead.

"Well, why did she ask if she didn't care about the answer?" I shouted, throwing my ghostly hands up.

Graves at least pretended to cover up his laugh. Shepard didn't bother.

"You know, if our roles were reversed, I'd at least have the decency to not enjoy it quite so much."

"Doubtful," Shep said with a smirk.

Scowling, I touched my body.

This time Esme did some kind of flying spin, unleashing two ninja stars and taking Graves and me out at the same time.

Shep was waiting for us, holding up nine fingers like some kind of spectral Olympic judge.

"Wait until I tell Esme you only gave her a nine."

Shep made a face. "Please. That was for you. Esme is tens across the board."

"You're rating my dying?"

He nodded. "You need to work on your dismount."

"Oh, fuck off," I said, but there was no heat in it. If I had to keep dying, at least my brother was here to keep me entertained.

This time Esme gave us a curious look. "Any requests?"

I blinked at her. "Uh . . . no? What kind of question is that?"

She shrugged. "Suit yourself." Then she twisted around and proceeded to lift a grenade.

"Whoa, Esme! Let's not destroy the house," I shouted in panic.

Esme pouted and set it down.

Graves was laughing beside me.

"You think this is funny?"

"Only your aunt would have a grenade handy."

A dart hit me in the neck, and my knees gave out as the world blurred. I couldn't even manage to form words before I slumped over into the darkness.

I lost count of the times Graves and I bounced between realms. The number of ways I'd died had blurred together, time losing all meaning as Esme killed us on a seemingly endless loop.

At some point, the very long night had ended. Sunlight peeked through the blood-spattered drapes of the living. I bent at the waist—in my living form, my breaths coming hard and heavy.

Dying was fucking exhausting.

Even Esme was starting to slow down a little, dark circles lining her eyes.

"How many times is that?" I huffed.

My aunt shrugged, digging through her weapons to find something she hadn't used to kill me and Graves yet.

"One hundred and thirty-six," Shep supplied from the sidelines. He sat with a tub of popcorn in the chair that I never actually made it to sitting on, reminding me of Aurora.

"A hundred and thirty-six?" I asked. "How the fuck have I not leveled up yet?"

"How do you know you haven't leveled up?" Shep asked, tossing another piece in his mouth.

"I don't feel any different . . ."

"Did you feel different the other times you came back?" he asked.

"Not really."

He stood, and the popcorn disappeared. "So you don't know if you've leveled up, then," Shep said. "I'm willing to bet you have. When we first started, it took fifteen minutes for you to show back up after Esme killed you. It started being instant somewhere around the twentieth death."

My mouth dropped open. "So I've been leveling up this whole time? And you didn't say anything?"

Exhaustion and just a little bit of annoyance bled into my tone.

"I figured if that's where you were at after twenty, you'd be a real badass after a hundred more."

"Oh, for fuck's sake," I groaned. "Esme, you can stop. I need to see what I can—"

I didn't get to finish that sentence before Esme said, "Fuck it. I won't get another chance to see what this does anytime soon."

I opened my mouth to ask what she was talking about when something rolled across the hardwood floors. It came to stop in between Graves and me.

Esme was already bolting for the other side of the living room when a slew of curses left my lips.

"Goddamnit! I told you not to use grenades in the house!"

Boom.

Red engulfed me, but pain didn't even get to register before I was back in the spirit realm.

Our entire fucking living room was destroyed because she wanted to try a grenade.

On either side of me, Graves and Shepard laughed like they didn't have a single care in the world.

"Seriously?" I demanded. "Why are you two laughing? I told her not to do that," I growled. A buzzing had started in my head, followed by the pounding of a headache that didn't go away no matter how many times I died.

Frustration at myself, at the situation, at the impossibility that I could ever defeat Thana mounted. Exhaustion from lack of sleep and dying on an endless loop was beginning to eat at me.

More than anything, though, I was hungry.

And Esme just blew part of our fucking kitchen to smithereens.

The tension in me snapped, and I lashed out.

"Stop laughing!" I shouted, smacking my brother in the chest. "I get that you're dead, but unless I can find a way to fix this, every person I care about will follow. This is serious, Shepard."

"Salem—" Graves started.

"Don't 'Salem' me," I growled. "You're just as bad right now."

"Look—"

"You look," I bit back. My jaw popping as I wheeled on him. "I get that I asked to die, and this is all my fault, but I'm tired, Graves. Exhausted. Can you guys just keep the fucking snickering to yourselves for two damn seconds—"

"Shepard?" My aunt's voice sounded different.

I paused in my ranting and blinked.

My hand wasn't incorporeal anymore. It was solid.

I'd never touched my body though . . .

"Esme?" my brother asked, looking shocked. "You can see me?"

My aunt stared at Shepard with a look of awe on her face for all of two seconds before she launched herself at him.

Shepard caught her around the waist and lifted her easily, swinging her around as he hugged her.

"My god is it good to see you again," Esme breathed, pulling back to look at him. She pressed her hand to his cheek, tears spilling down her face.

"You too, Aunt Esme."

My aunt smacked him on the arm with her free hand. "Don't you ever go and do something as stupid as getting yourself killed, ever again."

She was one to talk after chucking a fucking grenade in the house.

"Unless your sister is around," she amended.

"I could say the same to you," he replied with a slight smile.

I was still struggling to make sense of what was happening. It might have been the exhaustion fogging my mind, but without even trying, I'd managed to bring Shep back. Not just Shepard, but all three of us.

I blinked at Graves; he was grinning at me.

"You did it."

"I did it," I repeated, feeling a bit numb. *Holy shit.* "I wonder what else I can do . . ."

Before the thought was even fully voiced, my aunt, Shepard, Graves, and I popped into the spirit world.

Esme looked around with wide eyes while Shep let out a soft groan. "Not again."

"No, no, you aren't dead," I assured him. "It was me. I did it."

I let out a surprised laugh and then threw my arms around Graves, pulling all of us back into the destroyed remains of my living room. "I did it!"

He held me tight against the hard lines of his body. "Can we take it easy on the spirit melding thing for a while?" he asked with a tired laugh.

"Yes, sorry." I pulled back to look at my twin. The fact that he was here and very much alive finally penetrated the fog in my mind. It was my turn to throw myself at him, squeezing tight. "Welcome back."

He held me hard, stealing the breath from my lungs. Pulling back, he grinned and said, "About damn time."

I glared at him, but he waved me off as Graves moved in for a hug of his own.

"Good to see you on this side again, man," Graves said.

They did that manly one-arm slap thing and let each other go. "I think I've seen more than enough of you recently," my twin said pointedly, lifting his brows with a smirk.

"Hey! You said you didn't spy on us," I protested.

Shepard laughed. "I'm just teasing."

"You better be," I growled.

"Why would I want to see your pasty ass—"

"Hey, that's my girlfriend you're talking about."

Esme watched all of this with a happy grin, not bothering to wipe away the few tears that trickled down her cheeks.

"I'm sorry, I'm sorry. Man, not even a minute back and you two are already teaming up on me. Bitch me out later once I've finished saving your asses."

"Pretty sure that's the other way around," I said, crossing my arms.

Shep rolled his eyes. "Believe it or not, bringing me back really was a priority. There's something you need to know. Something I couldn't tell you in my other form."

"Why not?" Graves asked.

"Because the dead can't interfere." He gestured to his body. "Death told you that from the very beginning, and it's actually true. If I tried to interfere, I would have been sent to the afterworld instantly, and there's no coming back from that . . . but as I'm no longer dead, I can now tell you how to beat your bitchass other self."

"You know how to beat Thana?" I asked.

"She considers herself above humans and ghosts alike. She doesn't really think about what she says or how she acts, sort of like another person I know . . ."

I slapped him on the arm in good nature, but in truth, the comment sort of stung. Shep must have seen that because his expression softened. "I didn't mean to hurt your feelings, Squid. Thana is literally you, though. At least what you would have been had you led the life she did. She's literally a bad Salem, something that you guys seem to forget when really it's your biggest advantage."

"So you're saying our greatest advantage in handling her is thinking about how you would handle a four-hundred-year-old me with psychotic tendencies?"

Shep grinned. "That's exactly what I'm saying."

Before I could say anything more, my stomach chose that moment to emit a loud growl.

Three pairs of eyes turned to me and I shrugged. "Dying is hungry work. Let's order a pizza—or five—and then Shep, you're going to tell us how to end this."

Their expressions sobered. There'd be time to celebrate and reminisce later. Right now, we still had much bigger problems on our hands.

Hey Sister, Soul Sister

"Are you sure you can do this?" Graves asked. His hands pressed against either side of my face, long fingers locking around the back of my neck. He brushed one of his thumbs over my cheekbone, worry setting his blue eyes aflame.

I took an unsteady breath.

"It's the only way," I whispered. "Richard needs more time, and if Thana really is that much like me—she's not going to sit around waiting in the makeshift prison much longer."

He pressed his lips together.

"I know, I know, it's just—you suck at lying."

In any other situation, it would have been funny.

But not this time. Not here. Or now.

"I do," I agreed. "But I'm going to have to make it believable real fast—because otherwise, we have nothing. If she suspects this, we're done—unless I kill her."

I knew what he thought about this. He'd rather I just took what Shep told us and used it to end her. The thing was—she'd come back. One day. She'd be reborn and maybe she'd be like me, without her memories. Maybe she'd grow up to be a better me. A kinder one. Less of an asshole.

But in doing that, I would still strip away who she was. *What* she was. (And who were we kidding? We'd be lucky if the reborn Thana didn't just start murdering people.) Not to mention the other rather complicated side effects of actually putting an immortal down.

No. We had to be smart about this, and I had to play my role perfectly.

"Just remember the safe word if you wanna pull out—"

"Meatloaf," I said. "I'll do anything for love, but I won't do that."

I grinned at him even though it was edged with sadness. This could all blow up in our faces. If Thana didn't act how I would . . . if Death wasn't who I thought they were . . .

But what could I say? I wanted the killing to stop.

Peace was doable, damnit. Even if it was the last thing I did here on Earth.

"Alright, you two, let's go over the plan," Shep said, strolling into my bedroom. He was dressed in his old clothes and had his hair slicked back. Where he managed to find the time to make himself look presentable while we were wargaming, I don't know.

"I'm going to go ghost and take Graves with me. He's our go-between," I started.

"And I'm going to stay out of the way for the most part, so Thana doesn't know what's up," Graves said.

"Good, now Richard said he needs at least a couple hours before—" Shep started, giving me the look. This was where the plan got a little tricky.

"I know. My job is to keep her away from the house until it's time."

"Even if we're in danger," he added.

I swallowed. "Even if you're in danger."

My brother smiled and wrapped me in a bear hug. "You got this, Squid. I believe in you. Now you just need to make the psychotic one believe you too."

I squeezed him back. "Easier said than done, but I'll find a way," I vowed—and I meant it.

I needed to fix this for everyone, but I couldn't fix a damn thing until Thana was gone.

For good.

"The mines are ready to blow in case any of those fuckers think of getting frisky too early," Esme said. She was wearing a hard hat and suspenders that looked absolutely ridiculous.

I'd ask what she meant about mines, but in truth, I didn't want to know. Besides, the genuine surprise would help me play my role better.

"Alright, we need to go before she gets too impatient," I said, patting my brother's shoulder. He released me and stepped back.

Esme winked and gave us a little wave.

I returned it and grabbed Graves' hand, slipping us fluidly into the spirit realm.

"You remember how travel works in this realm, right?" I asked, not quite ready to leave him behind.

He nodded. "Don't worry about me. Just be careful, Salem."

I snorted. "Careful is my middle name."

Graves raised a brow. "When have you ever been careful?"

"Good point." I sighed. "I won't fuck it up. There's too much at stake."

He gave me a small smile. "Go. We've got things handled on this end."

We shared one last look before Graves faded from view. One second we were standing beside each other in the grayed-out version of my house, and the next I was in Thana's cell.

I watched her for a moment, all sorts of conflicted emotions writhing in my stomach. I pushed them away, I didn't have time to process them, and I couldn't afford to get sidetracked. The performance of a lifetime was about to begin.

Thana was seated on a little cot, her booted feet kicked up and crossed at the ankles. She sat with her arms folded over her chest, glaring at a guard who was on the phone at a desk just past her cell.

The reaper guard was a problem, but only a minor one. I couldn't risk popping into being with him right there, which meant I was going with option B. Jailbreak—well, sort of.

I reached out my hand and grasped Thana around the shoulder yanking her back and into the spirit realm.

She made the shift easily, toppling off her cot in one world and landing on the floor of the other. Bonus, since he hadn't heard her fall, the guard was unaware that his prisoner was now missing. He'd figure it out eventually, which was part of the plan, but the longer it took him to realize it, the better.

Thana stood, patting invisible dust off her legs, before finally lifting her face and looking at me. If she was surprised to see me, there was no trace of it in her expression.

"What, no hello?" I asked. "Not even after I came and broke you out?"

Thana laughed. "I could have left anytime I wanted to, and you know it."

"So why didn't you?"

"I was waiting for you," she said with a loose shrug, as if it should have been obvious. "Took you longer than I thought to come for me. I was just about to give up on you."

"Yeah, well . . . it's not easy to come and go when people think you're in jail. Made it a little tricky for me to take care of things on my end."

Thana smirked. "If you'd just let go of your mortal attachments, you'd realize it's not hard at all. Look at us now," she said, waving her arm for emphasis.

This was it. My opening.

I forced myself to look her straight in the eyes. "You're right."

Thana blinked. "Excuse me?"

Oh shit. I hoped that was just her surprise talking.

I took a deep breath and jumped right in. Embracing my inner psycho liar. I was a shit liar, the only way I was going to make this work is if I at least tried to see it her way.

"I said, you were right. About all of it. Graves, the reapers . . ." I trailed off and shrugged. "Everything."

Her brows lowered, and she looked at me skeptically. "Excuse me if I don't buy your sudden change of heart."

"I don't see why you wouldn't. I mean . . . wasn't that the point of all of this? To prove that in the end it's only me and you?"

She frowned. "Well, yeah . . . but after everything I've done, you don't just suddenly come to that conclusion, Salem."

I tried not to swallow. My skin felt hot. I was itchy all over trying to force myself into a role I was struggling to play, but people depended on me.

I had to do this.

"Excuse me if I'm not exactly thrilled that everyone in my life turned on me," I snapped back, feeding my inner bitch. If the liar couldn't pull this off, asshole Salem was my next best shot. "I mean, *I* didn't do shit, and they all just fell for it. No one would even give me a chance to explain. So yeah—I'm done with it. Done with them. If they don't want me, then they don't need me to save their asses. They can learn to save themselves."

It wasn't nearly as hard to pull off this version of me. I was angry. Resentful.

They really didn't believe me. And when this was all done, they probably wouldn't give me the time of day.

Part of me was pissed and thought they should handle the fallout on their own.

The rest of me saw the bigger picture and acknowledged the role I played.

"Alright." Thana nodded. "Let's take a walk. Have a little *fun*."

The way she said it made my stomach drop. I knew without a shadow of a doubt that people were going to hurt in my quest to make Thana believe I was leaving my old life behind.

That was something I had to accept, and hope that I could fix it later too.

"Where to?" I asked flippantly.

"Let's pay those reapers a visit. You were fond of them even though they treated you like garbage. It's time we put them in their place," Thana said.

The Brotherhood . . . there were worse places for her to start. Not many, but some. At least she hadn't wanted to go after Esme. Getting out of that without seeming suspicious would have been tricky.

"What do you have in mind?" I asked.

Thana lifted one delicate, blood-smeared shoulder. The dark look in her eyes made me wonder how I ever thought we could have a real relationship. I'd never actually trusted her, but still. Part of me was a bit angry about losing the chance to have a relationship with her, and then realizing that I was mad about it, I became angry at myself for feeling that way to begin with.

"Just a little game," she said, vaguely. I had the feeling that it wasn't going to be little, and that she was the only one who would think it was a game.

My stomach twisted, but I forced the words from my mouth. "I'm down."

She walked through the bars of the jail and came to a stop in front of her jailer before popping back into existence.

"What the—" The reaper tried to scramble to his feet.

Thana tsked, grabbing him by the flannel shirt and

lifting his entire body as if he were a teddy bear and not a two-hundred-pound guy.

Without further ado, she popped back into the spirit realm with him.

I had to work not to grit my teeth. That bitch knew how to take people in and out.

Fucking liar.

When she turned to look back at me, something devious shone in her eyes, but I simply waved her on as if bored.

She frowned, clearly not liking that.

Without more dramatics, she turned and tossed the reaper's spirit form into the jail cell.

His body popped back into the living world just before he hit the hard concrete floor.

Aw fuck.

My fingers twitched, but I didn't move. Instead, I looked away from the guy as if he were nothing.

"I thought you had something more interesting in mind," I said in an apathetic tone that mimicked her own.

Thana's eyes narrowed. "You want more? Fine. Let's go."

She spun around, grabbing my hand and pulling me along with her. I allowed myself one second to close my eyes and pray that I didn't just make things worse.

When I opened them, we were standing in front of a house I didn't recognize.

"Where are we?" I asked, in that same bored voice.

"Gamma Rho's new hangout. The boys needed somewhere to go now that their house is little more than ash and rubble."

I fought hard to keep my expression neutral. "Perfect."

She eyed me for a second before smiling. It was a dark, cruel thing, and I knew she was just getting started. "Let's thin the herd some more, shall we?"

So much for not making things worse. I took a deep breath and nodded, reminding myself that when all of this was over, I could bring them all back. This was temporary, just a performance.

Whether or not they'd forgive me when it was over? Well . . . you couldn't win them all.

We walked through the door into a living room where three reapers were resting in front of a flatscreen. I recognized Dale and Randy, and I thought the third guy was named Leo.

Without warning, Thana reached out, closing her hand into a fist and yanking it backward. When the bodies didn't move, I let out a breath I hadn't known I was holding, only to realize that I'd let myself relax too soon.

Standing around us in a loose semi-circle were the souls of the three reapers.

She'd killed all of them.

"Salem?" Randy asked, looking confused. "What happened?"

"Yeah, Salem?" Thana said, crossing her arms and grinning at me. "Why don't you fill them in."

"Why are there two of you?" Dale asked.

Randy blinked at me, giving me a confused smile like he was waiting for me to let him in on the joke.

"Payback," I said, my voice ice cold. I was holding onto my anger and feelings of betrayal in a death grip, using them to get me through this. It was easier than I thought it would be.

"For what?" Randy asked, looking hurt.

"It wasn't enough that you got most of us killed yester-day?" Leo added with a sneer.

Temper I could totally deal with. I didn't even have to fake the iciness of my response this time.

"Oh that wasn't me," I said, jutting a thumb at Thana. "That was my sister. I'm here now because you were all so quick to believe the worst in me. After everything I did for you guys, you wasted no time seeing me as the villain. So fine. Villain it is."

"Salem," Dale said, "wait. Isn't this a little over the top?"

"Over the top? After I brought all of you back to life? After you'd locked me up and didn't believe in me when I tried to warn you the first time? How many times do I have to prove myself?"

"Salem," he tried again.

"No. It's too late. You had your chance—more than one—and you blew it. So this time, you can fuck right off. Who's next?" I asked, turning to Thana and using the move to hide the fact that I couldn't bear to see the shattered look on Randy's face.

"Hmm," Thana hummed. She tapped her index finger against her lips. "We could go after the rest of the reapers . . ." she started. My chest clenched. "But I have an even better idea."

Judging by the devilish smirk on her face, what she considered to be 'better' was a matter of debate.

"What's that?" I asked, ignoring the reapers who were

now hurling insults in my direction. They stung, and I used that as armor for what was to come.

"I think it's time we paid a visit to that best friend of yours. What was her name again? Tara, Tamara—"

"Tamsin," I whispered.

"That's it," Thana said, nodding with approval. "Let's go see what she's up to. She did call us all sorts of names after her poor mommy died. She was simply heartbroken with what you'd done. I wonder how she'll feel when she realizes you're free."

I swallowed thickly, sweat coating my palms.

I knew this was a possibility. Shep warned me she would want to test me and that she'd go after anyone if it meant getting her way. She was me after all.

A bad Salem.

Now I had to make sure she didn't realize just how alike we were, and that I would do anything to protect the people I loved.

Even if it meant hurting them.

Gooood Salem

ONE MOMENT we were standing there, in front of the reapers she'd killed—the next we were at town hall. I recognized the meeting room as the one the Council used.

They were here now, and this was nothing like any meeting that had come before it.

Chairs were toppled over. The long wooden desk had been split down the middle, both ends leaning in where the centerpieces hit the floor, as if someone had been thrown on it. Based on the mob of supernaturals surrounding the raised platform, that wasn't exactly a long shot.

Dom stood off to one side, trying to reason with the members of the Council.

No one seemed particularly interested in listening, except perhaps the witches.

Tam stood a few feet away, thinking heavy thoughts. Her black eyebrows were pushed together, a pucker formed between them. She was without makeup, something that *never* happened. I mean, she was gorgeous without it, but my best friend was also a little vain.

It was more telling of the emotional turbulence within her than anything else.

"You lied to us. This is grounds for having you removed from the Council entirely," Nocturna was saying.

"I didn't lie about a thing," Dom replied.

"Then why is the reaper that turned on you in custody?" the vampire representative, whose name I'd forgotten, asked.

"It's complicated. This whole thing is complicated. We should just take a breath and start at the beginning—"

"She turned on us!" a reaper on the sidelines yelled. It was an older gentleman that I hadn't seen since the vote when Dom was elected.

"Shut up, Scythe. We'll deal with whoever that thing was—"

"What are you talking about?" Nocturna asked, holding her hand up to the angry mob for silence.

"I don't know who the fuck that girl was, but she wasn't Salem."

Beside me, Thana frowned. She did not like where this was going. Meanwhile, my heart swelled that Dom had seen through it. Him. Of all people. Maybe there was hope for the reapers after all . . .

"What makes you say that?" the she-wolf Serena asked.

Dom let out a callous laugh. "Salem is an asshole. She says a lot of dickish things, and she acts like a brat all the fucking time. I don't know how Graves puts up with her—"

"Can you get to the point?" Nocturna interrupted.

"She'd never lie like that. She's incapable of lying, even when it would save her ass. She once admitted to kidnapping someone. No. I don't know what that girl was, but it wasn't Salem. I put her in a holding cell until I can figure it out."

One for Dom. Zero for Thana.

Mentally, I was doing a little happy dance and knowing I was right to vote for his ass, however, Thana couldn't see that. So I kept my face stoic.

"He's lying!" someone from the crowd shouted.

"How do you explain Gerard?" Serena asked.

Nocturna cut her off. "We're getting offtrack. The wolf's death is not the matter currently before the Council."

Serena seethed, her skin rippling like she was fighting against the change.

"As entertaining as all of this is," Thana purred, "I think it's time we have a little fun with the succubus."

A protest was on my lips, but I swallowed it back, hating that Tamsin was getting pulled into this, but knowing now was not the time to back down. I had to keep Thana distracted. I had to make her believe I was on her side.

"How do you suggest we do that? She's on the Council. They're going to notice if she suddenly disappears in the middle of such a public meeting."

Thana tapped a finger on her lips, debating. "True, but creating a little chaos isn't exactly a bad thing."

I shrugged, not seeing an obvious way around it. "Your call."

"No, Salem, I think this one should be on you," she said, smiling like she'd caught me.

In a way, she had. She was calling my bluff. Would I really turn against Tamsin to prove my loyalty to Thana?

I scanned the restless crowd, wishing for a moment there was a way to cause a distraction that would at least let me remove Tamsin from the room without sending everyone into a panic.

Wait. Maybe there was a way.

Thana had mentioned we could control ghosts. With Shep currently out of the picture, and the Grimm ghosts not actually being ghosts . . . there weren't many people I could think of to call on.

"Tick tock, Salem."

I gritted my teeth. Alright, if I couldn't think of a ghost to summon, maybe I could just make these people believe there was one. I should've been able to fake a ghost attack . . . right?

Without any real idea what I was doing—which, let's face it, was pretty much how I did everything—I stared hard at the broken table and flicked my finger out, sending it flying into the wall and shattering.

People screamed, and everyone looked in the direction of the flying table.

"Oh, very nicely done. Looks like my big sister learned some new tricks while I was locked up."

"People weren't very happy with me." I shrugged. "You grab her while I keep their attention elsewhere," I muttered, already sending a few chairs flying across the room.

"What the fuck is happening?" Rembrandt asked, ducking as a broken chair headed straight at him.

"I think we're under attack!" Nocturna shrieked.

More screams rang out, but I barely heard them. I was wholly focused on one incredibly pissed-off voice.

"Salem Kaine, what the fuck are you doing?" Tamsin said, pulling free of Thana's hold. I could see the question burning in her eyes. She wasn't sure if this was part of my plan or not.

That little bit of doubt stung.

"So what do you think, Salem?" Thana asked. "Should we kill her?" my doppelgänger asked, running a ghostly hand down her cheek. Tamsin flinched. "We could play with her. Make her a little doll that walks and talks and does whatever we say?"

Fear shone in Tamsin's eyes.

"W-what's going on?" she stuttered.

"You, my little succubus, lost your faith too easily. Now my sister here has decided to let go of her humanity. She realized that things are more fun on this side of the line." Thana's lips curled up in a cold grin.

The color drained from Tamsin's face. At least, as much as it could, given she wasn't exactly corporeal right now.

I read her expression as clear as day, and it broke my heart.

"So what'll it be, Salem?" Thana declared.

In the living realm, the shouts had slowed. People were noticing that one of the seven Council members was missing. That she'd vanished into thin air.

"Where did Tamsin go?" the warlock representative asked.

No one seemed to have an answer.

I swallowed.

"I-I—" The words wouldn't come. Even with the world

as I knew on the line, I couldn't betray my best friend like this. I'd sworn I'd fix this, but even that I was going to fail.

Any apathy I'd managed to hold onto slipped from my face as the lie stalled on my lips, frozen by pain.

Thana waited several seconds and then smiled even brighter. Crueler.

She tossed her head back and laughed. The sound chilled me to the bone.

"I fucking knew it," Thana said, her laughter stopping as quickly as it had started. "You don't have it in you."

She tossed Tamsin aside and wiped her hands on her faded skinny jeans, as if disgusted by my friend's mere touch.

"Well—I—I said I was done, I didn't say I wanted to torture everyone." I scrambled to recover, but judging by the look on Thana's face, I was doing a piss-poor job.

"You can drop the act, Salem." She folded her arms over her chest. "I've been alive over four hundred years, and I've known you in every life you've led. Even when you could lie, it never got past me."

I let out a tight breath. "Fine. What do you want, Thana? You fucked up my life here. You've made it clear you want an eternal Bonnie to your Clyde. What is it that I need to give you for you to leave me the fuck alone and stop ruining people's lives?"

Any amusement on her face faded away into the cold lethal predator that sat below the surface.

"I want the same thing I've always wanted," Thana whispered. "A friend. A partner. You created me because you were lonely. I come back to you because I am too. Just like in that first life, though, you choose *them*. You may not choose death, but you always choose your human pets. Every fucking time. Even when you don't choose Death, you *never* choose me."

Behind her, Graves appeared. He gave me a single nod and then vanished before she even knew he was there.

The trap was ready. Now I had to find a way to get her there.

"You kill me in every life," I replied. "Of course I don't."

"Oh? Learned about that, did you?" she said, not even showing regret.

I laughed once, but it was devoid of humor. "No, actually. I suspected, though, and you just confirmed it. So much for knowing everything about me."

Once I knew who Death was and that they hadn't tried to kill me even though they'd found me—well, it didn't take long to start to wonder about that. And thinking on the fact I'd died in every life. At the end of it, there was only one logical conclusion. It all started and ended with Thana.

She narrowed her eyes.

"I kill you because you're a fucking idiot every time, and instead of leaving all this bullshit behind, you end up thinking that you can save it—save me—save Death." She groaned. "If you weren't me, I would have sent you to the afterworld by now. There are no other immortals on this plane, though—not outside you and Death—and between the two of you, I prefer the one that's stupid."

It would have hurt my feelings if I didn't already know she thought this way. I planned to use that to my advantage.

"So if you kill me in every life, why haven't you this

time? Why go to the trouble of trying to befriend me and getting me to see your side?"

Thana looked away. She was hiding something, or trying to.

"You might be stupid, but having a stupid twin is better than having no one at all. Not when the afterworld claims everything eventually—and while you were raised there— we aren't welcome there. Far from it, in fact."

I studied her features. The slight tremor in her bottom lip. The gleam in her gray eyes. She was good, very good.

But not good enough.

"That's only part of it." When Thana didn't respond, I shrugged. "Don't want to tell me? Fine. Hard to get what you want when you don't tell me anything, though . . ."

My heart sped up. This was working out perfectly. Exactly as Shep said. Now she just needed to take the bait . .
.

I turned like I was walking away.

"Wait."

I paused, trying to keep the smile off my face.

"Yes?" I asked lightly.

"I need your help," she uttered through gritted teeth.

"Mhm, I'm aware." I turned back, giving her my full attention again. "What I'm not aware of is why I should help you do anything after what you've done."

Anger flashed in her features, but she schooled it quickly.

"Death is coming for me. I've managed to evade it for centuries, but it's getting smarter. I can sense that it's here, I just can't figure out where or who. I need you to help me get rid of it. Permanently."

This time, I sensed the truth. Or most of it.

"How do we go about that?"

"Why on Earth would I tell you when you're looking to betray me?" she sneered.

I lifted a brow, and Thana seemed to check herself.

"Fine, even better question—give me a reason to help you," I said.

Thana looked from me, to the room of supes, to Tamsin's ghost—who was watching us silently.

I knew what she was going to say before she did.

"Help me and I'll leave your pets be," she said through gritted teeth.

"Prove it," I replied in a hard voice. I thrust my chin in Tamsin's direction. "Put her back."

Thana waved a hand, and Tamsin reappeared in the living world. It was just the two of us now.

"Happy?" Thana asked.

"Not a chance," I answered. "But it'll do."

Thana's brow furrowed. "So are you going to help me?"

"Unfortunately, yes. Death clearly hasn't done me any favors, and if this gets you both to leave me and the rest of Farrow's Square the fuck alone, then I'll do it."

I phased out of the Council room right as a group of reapers burst in. One of them was the dude Thana locked in a cell. Damn. They moved fast. I needed to be faster.

Reappearing at my house, I found the Hostess cupcake package sitting on the new dining room table. The living room was still destroyed, as was most of the kitchen. We'd moved a dining table up to the main room, so that Richard had time to work.

Judging by the fact that the cupcakes were sitting there

—and neither my aunt, my brother, or the warlock himself were around—the plan was truly in place.

Thana appeared behind me.

"What are we doing here?"

I took a deep breath and picked up one of the cupcakes. This was probably the last food I'd get to eat ever. That thought was depressing.

I tried to hold out hope that the second, sketchier half of this whole dealio would work. But there was no way to predict Death.

Without further delay, I picked up the cupcake and bit in.

It tasted as amazing as always. I hummed under my breath, and my skin lit up.

"Salem, what the fuck—"

"Shh," I snapped at her. "Don't ruin this for me."

I ate the other half of my cupcake, swallowing it down. When it hit the spot, I turned and said simply, "Welcome to forever with me, Thana. You're getting exactly what you want."

"What are you talking about?" She looked around, still not understanding. Not that I blamed her.

"It's you and me, trapped here in this house for all eternity. Congrats, Sis. I hope you like eighties music because we'll be listening to a lot of it."

Panic crossed her features. She tried to ghost away, and an invisible barrier stopped her. Her spirit rebounded back, slamming into the already ruined living room.

"I don't understand," Thana started. "How the fuck is this possible?"

"Trust my Aunt Esme to always know a way. Her fuck

buddy is a high warlock that perfected the equipment that allowed her to trap a ghost. When you ruined my life and started killing people, it gave me the bright idea—what if I could trap an immortal? Well. Turns out, I can." I motioned to the house. "My entire mansion has been spelled to contain us, and that cupcake I just ate triggered it. As long as I choose to stay in here, we're both trapped. Forever. Which means you can't ruin anyone else's life."

"No. You can't do this." She was frantic, spinning around and trying to ghost away, only to bounce off the invisible barriers time and again.

As I watched her, a true smile stretched across my face even as I myself was starting to panic a little inside. Where the fuck was Death?

"Let me go!" she screamed, hurling herself at me.

I caught her, our bodies flying through a coffee table as we landed on the ground surrounded by shards of wood and glass.

We struggled, rolling over, each one of us vying to be on top. Finally, I landed a punch to her kidney that seemed to knock the wind out of her long enough for me to pin her to the floor.

"Fight me all you want, Thana. You're not going anywhere."

She spat in my face. "I hate you. You're a pathetic excuse for a goddess. You never could see past the mortality of the humans you love so much and fully embrace what you are."

"If that means ending up like you, then I'm glad I never did. There's more to life than power, Thana. Maybe you would understand that if you actually allowed yourself to care about anything other than yourself."

She bared her teeth, struggling against my hold, but all those training sessions with Graves, plus my super-enhanced strength from dying a good hundred and forty times, made me more than a match for her.

When I didn't let her go, she went limp, her eyes going thoughtful. "What are those humans you love going to think when they realize that you've left them?"

I knew what she was trying to do, but she wasn't saying anything I hadn't already thought about myself.

With more bravado then I thought I possessed, I shrugged one shoulder, not letting on how much it would hurt if I miscalculated the last part of this plan and actually had to stay here forever. With her. Nope. I had to hold on. "They'll move on. It's what humans do."

"Some things people can never forgive," she said, her voice lashing out like a whip.

"Maybe not, but with time, hopefully they'll understand."

Thoughts of Graves' smoldering eyes, and my brother growing old, and Esme finding some new hobby to keep her young filled my mind, but I forced them away.

This wasn't the end. I had to believe that.

But either way, Thana was trapped and was no longer a threat. That was all that mattered.

"Well, well, well . . . isn't this an unexpected twist," a familiar voice said behind me.

Knock-Knock-Knockin' on Death's Door

MY CHEST EASED. Some of the inner panic draining away.

Death had come.

Finally.

"Where are your other bodies?" I asked, glancing over my shoulder.

Gretel stood in her lacy black dress, looking over the ruined remains of my living room.

Fucking grenade. I was still pissed about that one. If I was stuck here forever, I didn't even have a clean prison.

"They're about," Gretel answered vaguely. "Can't have all of me in one place for the wonder twins, can I?"

I chuckled. "You figured out what she wanted to do this time?"

Gretel surveyed Thana, who glared back. "It wasn't exactly a hard guess. In every life, she—or both of you—got rid of me. I wasn't taking any chances this time."

"What's she talking about, Salem?" Thana asked. For once she wasn't in the loop.

I was more than a little gleeful about that given how many times she referred to me as the 'stupid' twin.

"Meet Death," I said in response. "Or at least one of them."

Confusion clouded her gray eyes for a moment. I found it fascinating to watch. That's what I must have looked like ever since she came to town. Now the tables were turned.

She'd underestimated how far I would go in this life to save those I loved.

"*You're* Death?" Thana said incredulously. "But I killed Gretel a good two hundred years ago."

"Thana, Thana," Gretel shook her head. "You always overestimate yourself. I am Death, dear girl. I was never actually living. You ripped me apart and stuffed my soul inside living vessels to keep me from coming back—the same as you did with Salem. The difference is, where Salem's soul healed, and she was reborn—I was merely released every time one of those vessels died. After being ripped apart a few dozen times, though, I had this great idea. Really, I should have thought of it from the beginning. Perhaps you get that from me. We gods do tend to overestimate ourselves." Gretel smiled, and it reminded me a little too much of Thana.

"Get to the point," I groaned.

Gretel's eyes flashed, that ancient essence peering out at me.

"You're really no fun," she said, sounding like the twelve-year-old she appeared to be.

"She's really not," Thana muttered.

"Anyways," I said, interrupting them both. Since when was this a hate-on-Salem session? "Get to the point where you decided to not come back as a person but to exist as ghosts, pretending to be controlled by Death."

"Damnit, Salem," Gretel cursed. "You really know how to kill a punchline. I'm not fucking James. I've been at this for four centuries with you two and you couldn't let me have five minutes—"

"Provided that both of you and your stupid fucking games are why I'm trapped in here for eternity with her— no. I don't care. You died a few dozen times. So did I. Boo-hoo. You've hunted her this whole time because she's a fucking psycho, and she's hunted you in return. The only one that's even kind of blameless is me—"

Both Gretel and Thana went off.

"Are you fucking kidding me?" Thana demanded.

"You created her," Gretel said, motioning to my doppelgänger.

"Yeah, like four hundred years ago. The fact that you wanted her dead because I created her wasn't cool. You could have just gotten the fuck over it," I said, giving her the don't-fuck-with-me face. Seeing as how Death was ancient, they didn't seem to care.

"In creating her, you threw off the balance. The other gods were getting twitchy. They thought if one of my children could create other gods like this, what was to stop us, AKA you brats"—that was rich coming from a preteen's mouth—"and me, from having an army. There are conse-quences to everything, Salem, even for an immortal."

"Yeah, well, the last four hundred years have been us playing this game. You wanted her dead. It's not going to happen, and you know that. There's no way to truly kill her. The most we could do is reset her, and I'm not creating a whole new batch of reapers just to see if Thana two-point-oh is less fucked up."

"Hey!" Thana snapped.

"Oh, give me a break. You sat there calling me the stupid twin for like ten minutes when you thought I'd never figure it out. Death has been hanging around me ever since my first death. They clearly don't want me dead or I would be, which means someone else reset me. You're the only other being who could do that. The fact that you confirmed it without feeling even a hint of remorse—"

"Who wants their five minutes to get it out now," Gretel complained.

I turned my unamused face on her, crossing both my arms over my chest.

"You're right. We're all a little pissy about how things have gone. Killing her isn't an option, though, and resetting her isn't something I'm down for since it could lead us right back to this spot. You planned this whole thing. You watched me for months as I struggled to come into my powers. I have to think you're here for a reason and that there's a way to end this so we can all move the fuck on, and I don't have to trap us both for eternity."

Gretel watched me for a moment. Her red lips pursed together as she seemed to weigh me with her eyes.

"You're right. There is another solution . . .one that will fulfill the needs of all . . .parties involved."

"And you're just bringing this up now? How convenient," I said dryly, although I felt a little flutter of excitement at her words. This was exactly what I'd been hoping for. What were the odds this was all going to work out?

Slim was the answer. Especially considering my batting average, but hey . . . fingers crossed.

"I can still change my mind," she said, the threat heavy in her voice.

"I'm all ears, Not-Morticia," I said, barely suppressing my smile at her slight eye twitch. Maybe it wasn't the best time to annoy Death, but I couldn't help myself. After all they and Thana had put me through, every little win counted.

"Does anyone care what I think?" Thana asked.

"Nope," I answered without sparing her a glance.

Gretel smirked at my immediate response. "What would you say if I told you I could ensure Thana never set foot in your realm again?"

I raised a brow. "Maybe it wasn't clear, but the whole goal of this was *not* to kill her—or reset her since killing is all relative now."

"Who said anything about killing her?"

I stared at Gretel for a beat, trying to sense any hint of deception, but there was none. "Alright, in that case, I'd say what the fuck are you waiting for?"

Gretel nodded, as if that's what she'd been expecting. "There's another realm, one that you both have access to— although not without being escorted by me."

"Another realm?"

"Clearly, you know that there are multiple realms that exist alongside each other. You've been passing through the living realm and the in-between for weeks now."

"Well, yeah. Obviously. It was more a question about what realm you were referring to. So far the only other one I know about is the afterlife."

"Ah, yes. My realm," Gretel said and smiled. "But no, that's not where I'd take her. I'm speaking of the god realm. There, Thana would be brought before the Sentinel, and it would be up to them to decide what becomes of her."

Thana was suspiciously silent during Death's explanation. I stole a glance at her, but her expression was blank.

I didn't buy it. This was her future we were discussing. She was hanging on every word. I'd stake my life on it.

"The Sentinel?" I asked.

"It's like your Council, but comprised of the original gods."

I pressed my lips together. This was sounding too good to be true. "And I have your word she will not be reset?"

Call it weakness. Call it strength. I didn't want Thana reset for two reasons. The first was that to do so, you had to stuff her in living creatures, therefore making them reapers. It was the actual way reapers were created originally. She realized my soul would heal itself, but it's hard to heal as me when I'm in tiny little pieces and grafted onto other souls.

A whole new batch of reapers was not the solution. Given what they could do, that kind of power shouldn't just be handed out to whoever.

The second reason was that resetting Thana wasn't guaranteed to fix her. She said that every life I came back, I still chose humans and Death. What if every life she was still a fucking psycho? James wasn't even a god and he killed so many people and ruined so many lives. Thana could do so much worse. No. I'd rather her be forced to work through her shit.

Become someone else. Someone better.

So yeah, resetting her was not in the cards if I had my way.

"You have my word. Is this satisfactory to you, Daughter?"

There was something really creepy about a twelve-year-old dead girl calling me daughter.

I was about to nod when another question occurred to me. "Why now?"

"What do you mean?" she asked, cocking her head.

"If this was a solution, why did you wait until now? This lifetime? If you could have done this centuries ago, why wait so long?"

"Ah, well, that's simple, really. I was waiting for you. Yes, I had a couple hundred years where I was split, and I couldn't do this without both of you together—but the reason we've been at this for so long is largely because I needed you."

"Me?"

"Haven't you realized it yet, Salem? This has been a test. All of it. I needed to be sure you were still worthy of the job you were created for."

That did not go over well.

I mean, I knew she'd been playing with me, but the thought that it was all some kind of science experiment had never crossed my mind.

I clenched my jaw, anger swelling. "You were fucking testing me?"

Gretel sighed. "Thana is clearly not suitable to be Death's Overseer on this—or any—realm. She abhors those she is supposed to watch over. You, however, were made for this purpose. I needed to ensure that had not been lost. I am pleased to find that it hasn't. The way that you place the lives of those you were designed to protect and serve above your own proves that you are still capable of carrying out your sacred duties."

She was using a lot of overinflated words that sounded a bit like static to me, but I got the gist of it. She'd been interviewing me for the job, and I'd passed.

"Well, your methods are crap, but I can't disagree with your assessment."

Gretel smiled. "Glad we have that all cleared up."

"So if you take her to this 'realm of the gods,' they'll decide what to do about her, but she won't come back here, ever?" I asked, wanting to make a hundred percent sure.

"She won't be able to. Only *true* gods can pass in and out of that realm. You both come from Death, and so *my* realm and that of the spirit world are open to you. But neither of you are true gods. You were still born of flesh— the hope there being that you would feel as humans feel, and therefore be able to do what you were meant to do."

"If taking her away is punishment for what she's done, why are you not punishing me?" I asked.

Gretel smiled. "By your account, I already have. Four hundred years and forty-something resets, you have finally figured it out. In letting you be reborn thinking you are human, you grew to love these humans, and in this life, the loss you've suffered made you strong enough for the trials I gave you."

"But why? Why go to all that trouble and not simply create another Daughter to do this?" I waved to the house around me.

"Because, *you* are my daughter. Every now and then one

of you acts out, but you don't simply end your children when they disobey. You teach them lessons. Help them learn from their mistakes."

There was something in her eyes, beyond the ancient, immortal gaze. Something not quite soft, but fond, nonetheless. Maybe true gods couldn't feel as humans can, or so she claimed, but I had to think they felt something.

"Besides," she continued. "The gods don't like it when I create new offspring. There's a system. Part of why this whole thing started to begin with." She gave me a meaningful look.

"You know, you may have created me, but I don't remember it, and after everything you've put me through, I don't like you very much."

Gretel didn't seem all that bothered by it. She simply shrugged and said, "If your kids don't tell you they hate you at some point, you probably haven't done your job very well. Though you think like a human, you are very much immortal. You'll get over it."

Ugh. Fucking parents. I forgot what that was like, though I really didn't see Gretel as a parent, nor Aurora or Rumpy for that matter.

She turned toward Thana. "Ready to go, cupcake?"

"Wait—" I said, stumbling forward.

"You know, for someone that complains about wanting me gone, you sure are dragging this out," Gretel griped.

"Thana said we can't go to the afterworld. That we're not welcome. Is that true?" I asked.

Gretel waved a hand. "You can, but I don't like you guys sticking around for too long. You have a job to do here, and time passes differently in my realm. You could spend a week there, and here it's been a year—or longer. Too much time there and your duties here are neglected. Speaking of, I'll be sending one of my assistants over from the afterworld to retrain you. Endeavor to not be reset again, if you can manage it. Retraining you takes forever, and my assistants hate being in this realm."

Well. That was better and worse than expected. Gretel started to walk away again, and I grabbed her arm.

"Will I see my dad again? My mom?"

"Salem," Gretel said, my name coming out like a sigh. "We'll set up a vacation for you—eventually. I've got other kids to deal with. It's been four hundred years, and while I can exist in multiple forms—frankly, it's fucking weird."

Out of nowhere, Rumpy, Aurora, and another twenty ghosts all popped up.

They were Death. All of them.

Gretel cast a sideways look at Thana. "Don't even get any ideas right now. Salem is finally where I need her to be, which means I can handle you."

Thana pressed her lips together. I couldn't read her expression easily, even though it was my own.

"Alright," Gretel called out. "Time to go." Aurora came to stand on one side of Thana and grabbed her upper arm. Rumpy went to stand on the other, doing the same.

"One more thing," I said.

"For fuck's sake—" Gretel started. Man, her accent fluctuated a lot. Gotta say, I preferred her being a creepy ghost to the reality, but I'd take what I could get.

I went to stand in front of my other half. Thana was avoiding my gaze, but that was alright. She didn't need to look at me for what I had to say.

"I hope that you find what you're looking for."

Her eyes snapped up to mine. "I don't need your fucking pity—"

"This isn't pity," I bit back. "After what you've done, you don't deserve pity. But you *are* me. Which means even though you're a shitty fucking person and you ruined any chance of a life where we were sisters—I do hope that in the end, you find your person. Whoever that will be. Find them and don't let your insecurities come between you. Don't push them away."

With that, I leaned forward and kissed her cheek. It was cold to the touch.

Shock permeated her features.

"It's time," Gretel said. "Release the trap, Salem."

I gave them a bittersweet smile. Only hours ago I was wagering whether I would get an eternity of imprisonment or not. Now, I had forever before me. But that didn't mean I was free.

Picking up the second cupcake on the table, I took a bite and walked right out where my front door should have been.

The barrier popped like a bubble. I sensed it, the moment they were gone.

An odd sort of peace filled me after all that had happened.

I stood on my lawn, eating my cupcake as the sun set.

A ghost of a touch made me shiver.

"You did it," Graves said. I looked down to see his fingers in their spirit form twined with mine.

"No," I said. "We did it. All of us."

Shit Meet Fan

STILL HOLDING ONTO GRAVES' hand, I gave a little tug and pulled him back into being. He glanced down.

"Never going to get used to that."

I gave him a tired smile. "I have to admit, it has its perks, though."

"Very true," he agreed, lifting a hand to brush some hair off my face. "So what's next?"

"Sleep. For like seven years. I'm—" But my words were cut off as the sound of angry voices reached me.

I narrowed my eyes and glanced down the driveway, seeing the crowd surging our way like some kind of human tidal wave.

"Are you fucking kidding me?" I groaned.

"At least they don't have pitchforks," Graves said.

"Not helping," I muttered, feeling like I was in no shape to face off against the entire supernatural community. Can't a girl get a break for two goddamn seconds?

"There she is!" a woman screamed, pointing at me.

The mob started racing faster.

Esme and Shepard raced around the corner of the mansion, coming from the direction of the pool house where they'd been hiding.

"What's going on?" Shepard asked, his eyes going wide at the hundreds of people pushing their way onto our property.

Esme, in news that surprised no one, looked eager.

"Esme . . . what did you do?" I asked.

A massive boom drowned out anything she might have said, sounding five times as loud with my enhanced hearing.

I'm pretty sure I shouted, my hands flying to my ringing ears as I caught the explosion of dirt and stone flying through the air, along with countless limbs.

Those not affected by Esme's mine paused, exchanging looks before regrouping and rushing forward again. Two more mines went off before they finally remained in place, content to shout their abuse at me from the driveway.

It felt like I was seeing double as the ghosts of those who hadn't survived Esme's boobytraps started to appear and hover around the fringes of the mob. Their voices were just as loud and irate as their living counterparts.

"Can everyone please just shut up!" I shouted, for all the good it did.

These people wanted blood, specifically my blood. As far as they were concerned, I was at fault for everything wrong in their lives. Hardly fair, considering I hadn't been around long enough to have caused the undercurrents of bigotry and resentment that were the source of their discontent, but every group of disenfranchised people needed a scapegoat, and the people of Farrow's Square had settled on me. It was the one thing it seemed they could all agree on.

Dom and Tamsin stepped forward, using their arms to bring the fuming crowd's shouts down to a dull roar.

I had to admit I was glad to see they'd both made it here unharmed.

"Salem, is that you?" Dom asked.

I crossed my arms and exchanged an incredulous look with Graves. "How does he expect me to answer that? If I wasn't me, it's not like I would admit it." I rolled my eyes. "You need to ask smarter questions, Fuckface."

Dom's lips curled down in a frown, and he sighed. "It's Kaine, alright."

I could still hear people calling for my execution, insisting that I was to blame, but for the moment, the Council seemed to be ignoring them.

"Care to explain yourself?" Nocturna asked, moving to stand on Dom's left side.

"Does it matter what I have to say?" I asked, my exhaustion robbing me of any patience I might have had.

"Salem—" Graves started..

"No, seriously. Does it matter? Because as far as I can tell, no matter how many times I've proved myself, you are all so quick to believe the worst about me."

A few of the faces I recognized near the front of the mob frowned and shifted uncomfortably.

"Can you blame us? When someone who looked exactly like you practically incited a riot?"

"Yeah, I can actually. Considering all I have been doing has been trying to prevent that exact thing from happening. I keep bringing people back to life—why would I suddenly pull a one-eighty?"

"What do you mean, bringing people back?" Nocturna looked from me to Dom. "What does she mean?"

"Salem isn't a reaper," Dom announced. "She's something more."

Murmurs started to swell behind him as the mob passed the news back.

"That isn't possible," Rembrandt said. "It would make her some kind of unknown supernatural."

"Not a supernatural," I corrected. "A goddess."

For a second, you could have heard a pin drop before laughter and snorts of derision filled the air.

"Yeah, right," a supe I didn't recognize said.

I narrowed my eyes. Completely over this bullshit. All I wanted was a nap. And a dozen cupcakes. And to be naked with Graves. I think I fucking earned it.

But no.

These fuckers needed proof.

Fine.

Closing my eyes, I focused on all the spots I'd seen the ghosts, and then focused on those souls. When I opened my eyes again, all of them were alive.

I couldn't quite contain my smirk at the sudden silence that little stunt had caused.

"What? Not quite enough proof for you? How about this?"

I started calling on those that I knew died during Thana's reign of terror. Summoning the ghosts that still lingered in this realm. I was fortunate that the vast majority of them weren't ready to go just yet.

They rematerialized in their ghostly forms, waiting silently for what I would do.

Without even a wave of my hands or blink of an eye, they turned corporeal, coming back to life in the flesh. One at a time, they popped back into existence, and soon, the area before me started to swell with the dead I'd brought back. I probably should have checked with Esme to make sure there were no more hidden mines, but it seemed she left the area closest to the house unarmed.

Sarah raced toward a sobbing Tamsin, wrapping her in her arms, before turning to me and mouthing, "Thank you."

Much better.

Thank you. That's what they should have been saying every time I brought someone's ass back. Instead I got an angry mob and sleep deprivation.

"Fucking twatwaffles," I muttered, crossing my arms over my chest.

"Want me to blow them up?" my aunt offered, coming up beside me. She turned around and pulled something that looked like a cross between a rifle and a cannon. At my gaping, Esme smiled. "Richard bought me a grenade launcher to show his appreciation." She winked, and Shep made a gagging sound. I was with him on that.

"I think we're good here," Shep told her.

Most of the crowd of supernaturals seemed to have recovered their shock at not being dead anymore, or at having their loved ones back. And for once, it didn't look like anyone wanted to kill me.

That was an upside, but the night was still young.

"So?" I called out over the barrier of dirt and rock and crumbled-up chunks of driveway that separated us. "Are we even, or do I need to put more of you back in the spirit realm just so you'll leave me the fuck alone? Because I'm exhausted, and really need some food, and then sleep."

And orgasms.

I left that one out since Esme was standing there and she was weird enough that she'd actually want to talk about it instead of being grossed out like she should be.

"If we weren't, would it really matter?" Nocturna asked, sending me the same question back I'd asked her. "You just brought the dead back without much effort at all. I get the feeling that whatever we do won't really affect you."

"Oh, it'll affect me," I said. "But I can't die, so more than anything, it'll just piss me off."

Graves ran his hand over his face, muttering something about me and knowing when to keep my mouth shut.

"Well then, Salem Kaine, it seems we're at an impasse," Nocturna said, projecting her voice over the thirty yards that separated us. "I, for one, don't wish to see any of my people dead."

"Nor I," Rembrandt added.

"The witches will abstain," the warlock representative added.

"As will the dwarves," the female dwarf added.

Tamsin pulled away from her mom long enough to say, "I never wanted you dead to begin with. Then again, I've known all along it isn't possible."

The tears of happiness on her cheeks were drying. There were words still left to say between us, but those were things for later. When everyone else was gone, and I was no longer swaying on my feet.

The only two left to comment were Dom and the she-wolf Serena.

The Fuckface stepped right up to the edge of the barrier.

I tensed.

"You fucked up, Kaine. But you also fixed it. I know a thing or two about that . . ." He trailed off, and I gathered this was as close to an apology as I was going to get from him. "For what it's worth, I never doubted you." He winked. "Not this time."

"I know," I said back. "I was at the Council meeting earlier. Looks like I voted for the right reaper to turn things around."

He grinned.

"What about Gerard?" Serena said.

I barely suppressed my groan. This bitch would not let this go.

"What about him?" I asked.

She gestured to the people milling around. "You brought everyone else back, and yet I don't see his face among the ranks of those given a second chance."

"I never wanted Gerard to die, and I'd never agreed with the Council's rationale behind why he deserved execution in the first place, but unlike the rest of—" I barely caught myself before I slipped and mentioned Thana's name, "the casualties, Gerard had been judged and sentenced by the supernatural community's chosen leaders. It didn't feel like my place to make the call."

Serena frowned, but she was the only one—at least as far as I could see. There were a lot of fucking people.

The rest of the Council, however, was looking at me

with begrudging respect. It was rare that I didn't just do whatever the fuck I wanted, but in this particular instance, leaving the people of Farrow's Square to deal with the consequences of their decision felt like the right choice.

"Have you changed your mind?" I asked, the challenge clear in my voice.

The Council members looked at each other, considering my question. Behind them, the supernaturals held their breaths.

"I think . . ." Dom started, blowing out a breath, "that if nothing else, the events of the last few days have proven that the way we've done things may no longer be the best fit for Farrow's Square. Perhaps it is time we reevaluate."

Tamsin grinned. "I second that suggestion."

"The kind of change you speak of, it isn't easy," the dwarf representative said.

"No, but we've seen what failure looks like now," Dom pointed out, gesturing at the destruction around them. "I think it is time for us to find a new way. Perhaps that change can start with giving Gerard a second chance. It does not correct what he did, but . . . many were given second chances today. Perhaps he deserves one was well."

"Am I hallucinating?" I asked Graves.

"No," he laughed. "This is really happening."

"Way to go, Dom," I said.

Nocturna looked less certain. "You are not the sole member of the Council," she said.

"For a change this big, maybe it's not the Council's decision to make. You're a fan of votes. Let's put it to the people," Tamsin said, spinning around to face the mass of supernaturals. "All in favor?"

I was the first to raise my hand, not that anyone was paying attention to me. The rest of the crowd was a little more hesitant. The wolves, obviously, were quick to agree, but then surprisingly more and more hands lifted in the air. Not all of them, but a clear majority.

Color me impressed. Maybe these assholes could learn from their mistakes after all.

"The people have spoken," Dom said, looking at Nocturna.

Her lips were pressed together, but she nodded. "So they have."

"Kaine! Do your thing."

We were going to have a talk about him bossing me around now that I was officially not under the reaper banner, but I'd let it go for now. Anything to get me closer to my bed . . . and my cupcakes.

I took a deep breath, mentally summoning Gerard. By the time I released my breath, Gerard was standing in front of me, looking stunned.

"What's going on?"

I gave him a smile. "They're giving you another chance. Don't fuck it up."

He swallowed, and then nodded before turning and shuffling over to embrace Serena.

"So, are we done here now?" I asked, the question aimed at Dom, but for everyone.

He nodded. "For now."

"Cool, get the fuck off my prop—wait, Esme"—I turned toward my aunt—"is it safe to go the way they came?"

She held a little device up. "I disarmed the rest of the mines. It's safe."

"Excellent." I looked back at Dom. "Kindly fuck off. I'm going to bed."

Without waiting for a response, or to see who followed me, I turned and went inside.

Happily Fucking Ever After

"That the last of it?" Graves called.

I poked my head out of the newly fixed front door. "Yup, that's the last of it."

The trunk slammed shut. In the back, all of our things were packed in tight. Well, all the things we needed. Graves and I were taking an extended road trip, along with my brother.

Where to?

The sunny coast of California.

It's where Shep's human boyfriend, Colin, ended up.

So, here I was being the most amazing sister and helping my newly undead brother get his happily ever after. Seemed only right since I got mine.

"I'm going to miss you," Tam said. Her thin brown arms wrapped tightly around my shoulders.

I hugged her back fiercely. "It's only a few months . . . probably."

Truth was that this trip was an excuse for me to get out of town. While over a month had passed since Thana's departure and things had calmed down a lot, there was still a lot to do. And frankly, I was tired of being called in to referee shit between supernaturals getting out of hand.

Graves finished his finals early and managed to pull Cs despite the amount of time he'd missed this last semester. You know what they say, though. Cs get degrees, and coming from two very wealthy families, we were going to be just fine.

Away from here.

"Yeah, yeah," Tamsin sighed. "I feel like I only just got you back." She pouted.

Graves chuckled. "We'll be back. Somehow I doubt Esme will let them both stay away too long this time."

"Don't worry too much about me." As if she'd heard him, which let's be real, she probably did, my aunt came up from the basement wearing a mosquito hat with net mesh that draped over her shoulders. She wore tan trousers and a thick, long-sleeved shirt with her combat boots.

"Esme," Shep sighed. "Why are you dressed like a shitty impersonation of Crocodile Dundee?"

She held up her left hand. In it, a machete with diamonds encrusted in the handle sparkled obnoxiously. *Oh no . . .*

"Richard proposed," she declared. "And I said yes. We're going on a jungle safari in the Amazon for the next two months now that they lifted the ban on supernaturals leaving Farrow's Square."

"Esme . . ." I said slowly, releasing Tamsin. "When you say you said yes—"

"We tied the knot this morning at the courthouse," my aunt said, then she leaned in to whisper conspiratorially, "and not the knot you're thinking of, although we tied that too. Richard is really great with rope—"

"Nope," I said loudly, turning and walking out the front door. "Can't do it. I love ya, Esme. Try not to die down there. It'll be a hot second before I can find you and bring you back."

The sound of my aunt laughing followed me out to the driveway where Graves was already waiting.

Shep was talking to Esme with a serious look on his face. I'm sure whatever last-minute lecture he was giving her was going in one ear and right out the other. Esme didn't take advice from anybody. Least of all the two of us.

Tamsin stood at the door, giving me a little wave and trying to hide the fact that she was sniffling. I blew her a kiss, a little more of the tension easing inside of me. Things weren't totally back to normal between us, but we were getting there. I think a little time would heal the rest of the wounds.

I leaned against the Impala, holding my hand out for the car keys without saying a word.

Graves eyed my hand, and I could feel his eyes drag up my arm as he looked from my palm to my face. I shivered; heat expanded inside of me as I imagined his lips traveling that same path. I wondered if it would always be that way between us. I certainly hoped so, given that forever was a long fucking time.

"You looking for a high five?" he asked, a small smile ghosting his very kissable lips.

"Nope. Give me my keys, Reaper."

"You think you're driving? With your track record?" he asked, raising a brow.

"I crashed *one* time," I groaned.

"And you died."

I held up a finger. "Which is no longer an issue, ergo . . ."

He mirrored my pose. "You're forgetting the part where you can bring back people, not cars. It's a long way to Cali, and I'm not making it in a rental."

I narrowed my eyes and glared at him.

Shep chose that moment to waltz over and snatched the keys out of Graves' other hand. "You're both wrong. In case you've forgotten, this is *my* car. I'll be driving."

My mouth fell open, and I stared at my twin as he eased around both of us and slid into the driver's seat. Well, shit.

"Graves gave it to me," I protested.

"Because I was dead, which I am not anymore. *Ergo*, the rights revert back to me."

"What kind of bullshit logic is that?" I asked, throwing up my hands and looking to Graves to back me up.

He was laughing and shook his head. "Nope, I'm staying out of this one. I love you both too much to pick a side."

"I'm going to remember that, you traitor," I told him. Looking at Shep, I said, "You'd think he'd side with the one who gives him blow jobs."

"He's not really my type, but it's not like—"

I held up my hands. "Annnnd that's enough of that. No one wants that mental image, thank you very much."

Shepard grinned, and I realized he'd done it on purpose to throw me offtrack.

"I'm not okay with this. You're a shit driver."

"Says the girl who totaled her car looking for a damn

cupcake. Just shut up and get in already. We're burning daylight."

I had to admit, Shep looked pretty cute in the driver's seat of the Impala, his hair tousled and his black Ray-Bans in place.

Maybe there was some kind of karma in Shep being the one to drive us out of here since he was the one I came back for in the first place.

"Fine." I threw up my hands and stepped around Graves, moving to claim shotgun before he got to it. "But if you crash, I'm going to make you kiss the ground I walk on before bringing your ass back."

"Yeah, yeah, we'll see about that. I could just haunt you until you bring me back. You're not much of an exhibitionist—"

"Ew, Shep," I complained as I hopped in the passenger seat. Graves climbed in the back, and Shepard threw it in reverse. I waved to Tamsin as we pulled around the driveway.

When we turned out on Mansion Lane, the giant 'S' filigree of the Shroud gates closed, and I couldn't help thinking that one chapter of my life was over.

The worst of it was past us now.

Shep was sitting next to me again, just like old times. Graves was at my back, and he would be forever. "Here We Go Again" was blaring on the radio as we flew down the highway. As the sign for Farrow's Square approached, I knew that while one chapter might be over, an even better one—and hopefully, much longer—was just beginning.

Eternity was a long fucking time.

Thankfully, I had someone to share it with—and Hostess cupcakes didn't have a real expiration date.

The End.

Text "Books" to (844) 506-1510
To stay up to date on future releases and sales!

If you want to connect more with Kel and her other readers, please join her Facebook Readers Group.

About Kel Carpenter

Kel Carpenter is a master of werdz. When she's not reading or writing, she's traveling the world, lovingly pestering her co-author, and spending time with her family. She is always on the search for good tacos and the best pizza. She resides in Maryland and desperately tries to avoid the traffic.

To keep up with Kel and her books, join her Facebook Group: www.facebook.com/groups/thecrowsnestread-ersguild/

Acknowledgments

What a rollercoaster it's been. Three books in four months split between two brains may not seem like a huge task, but when you factor in illness, the holidays, death in both families, and just the general unpredictability of life, this was one monumental undertaking. One we wouldn't have managed to accomplish without the strength of the other. A good co-author is equal parts therapist, cheerleader, and life partner. We were blessed to find all three in each other. #capygatorforlife

It's mystifying that we managed to do it at all, except that there was something so special about this project it became a sort of escape when everything else went to shit. Salem is magic that way. Or maybe it was Graves. Or Esme (let's be real, it was definitely Esme.) And the best part is, you guys love these characters as much as we do. As writers, we write because words are in our soul, but its' you—the readers—who give those words wings and bring our stories to life. Thank you for going on this insane journey with us.

A, Dom, alpha and beta readers thank you for being our support team. You guys are incredible.

And last but never least, to our husbands, thanks for letting us ignore you for hours at a time while we sent voice clips and text messages trying to sort out the mess our characters made. There were probably days we had crazed looks in our eyes and a maniac obsession with the voices in our heads—okay there were absolutely days like that—but you have been champs. Thank you for waiting patiently for your wives to return to you.

Until next time...

Kel & Meg